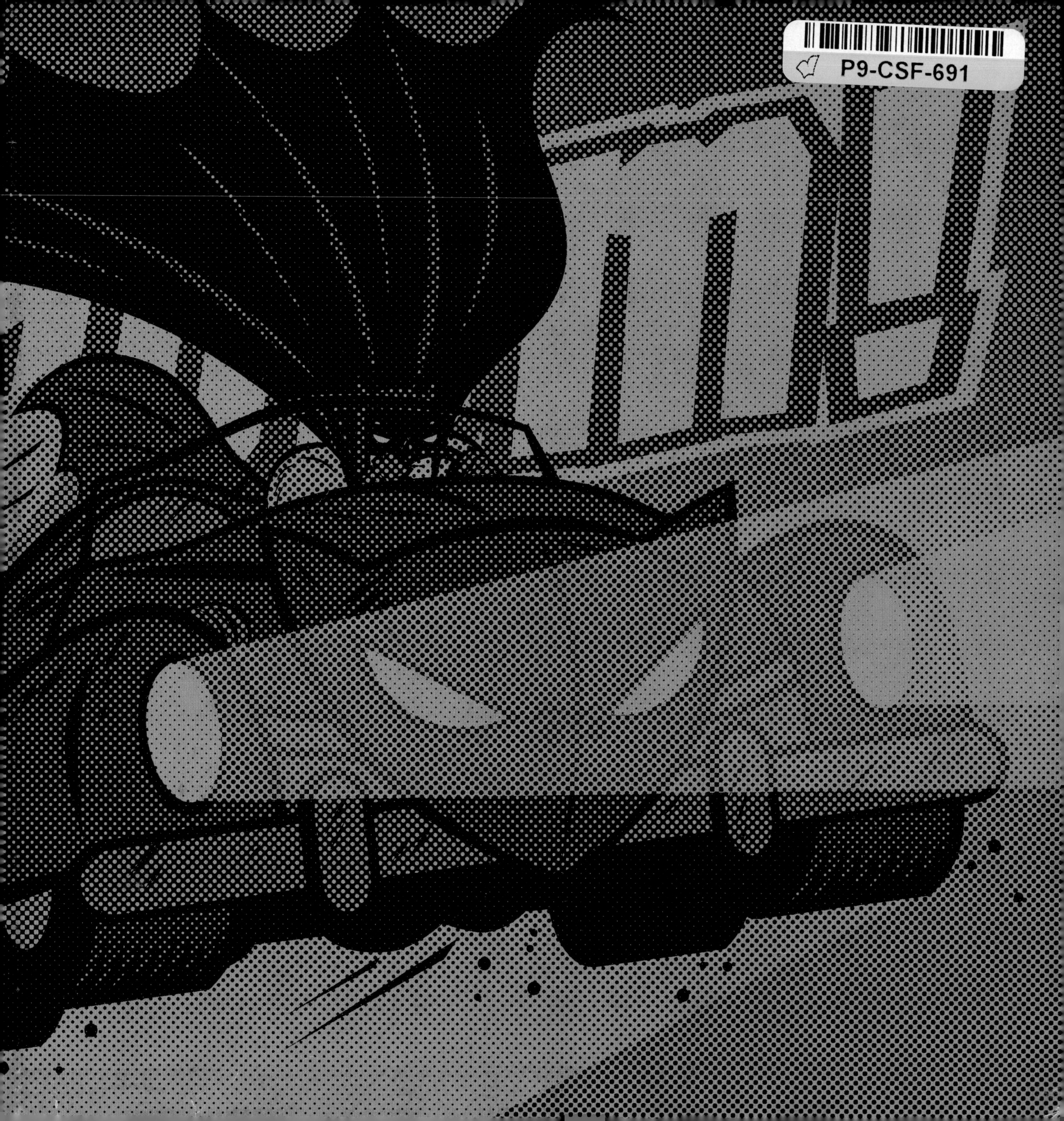

Dedicated to Bob Kane, Bill Finger, and Dick Sprang, along with the countless
other Batman artists who have given me a lifetime of inspiration.

A special dedication with gratitude to John Nee for his belief in my work
and to Russell Binder for his unrelenting support and friendship.

Big thanks to Joy Peskin, Jim Hoover, and Steve Korté for their patience and help.

Last but not least, a HUGE bat-thanks to my son Dante for his consummate support,
and for being my biggest, most cherished fan.

VIKING
Published by Penguin Group
Penguin Young Readers Group, 345 Hudson Street, New York, New York 10014, U.S.A.
Penguin Group (Canada), 90 Eglinton Avenue East, Suite 700, Toronto, Ontario, Canada M4P 2Y3
(a division of Pearson Penguin Canada Inc.)

Penguin Books Ltd, Registered Offices: 80 Strand, London WC2R 0RL, England

First published in 2008 by Viking, a division of Penguin Young Readers Group

10

LIBRARY OF CONGRESS CATALOGING-IN-PUBLICATION DATA IS AVAILABLE
ISBN: 978-0-670-06255-3

Manufactured in China   **Book design by Ralph Cosentino**   Set in Anime Ace

BATMAN

THE STORY OF THE DARK KNIGHT

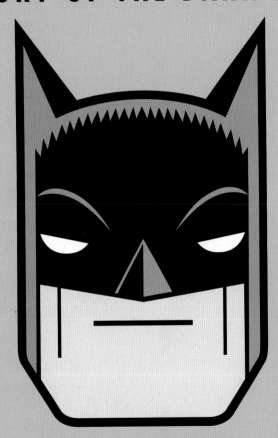

WRITTEN & ILLUSTRATED BY
Ralph Cosentino

VIKING

BATMAN CREATED BY BOB KANE

TM

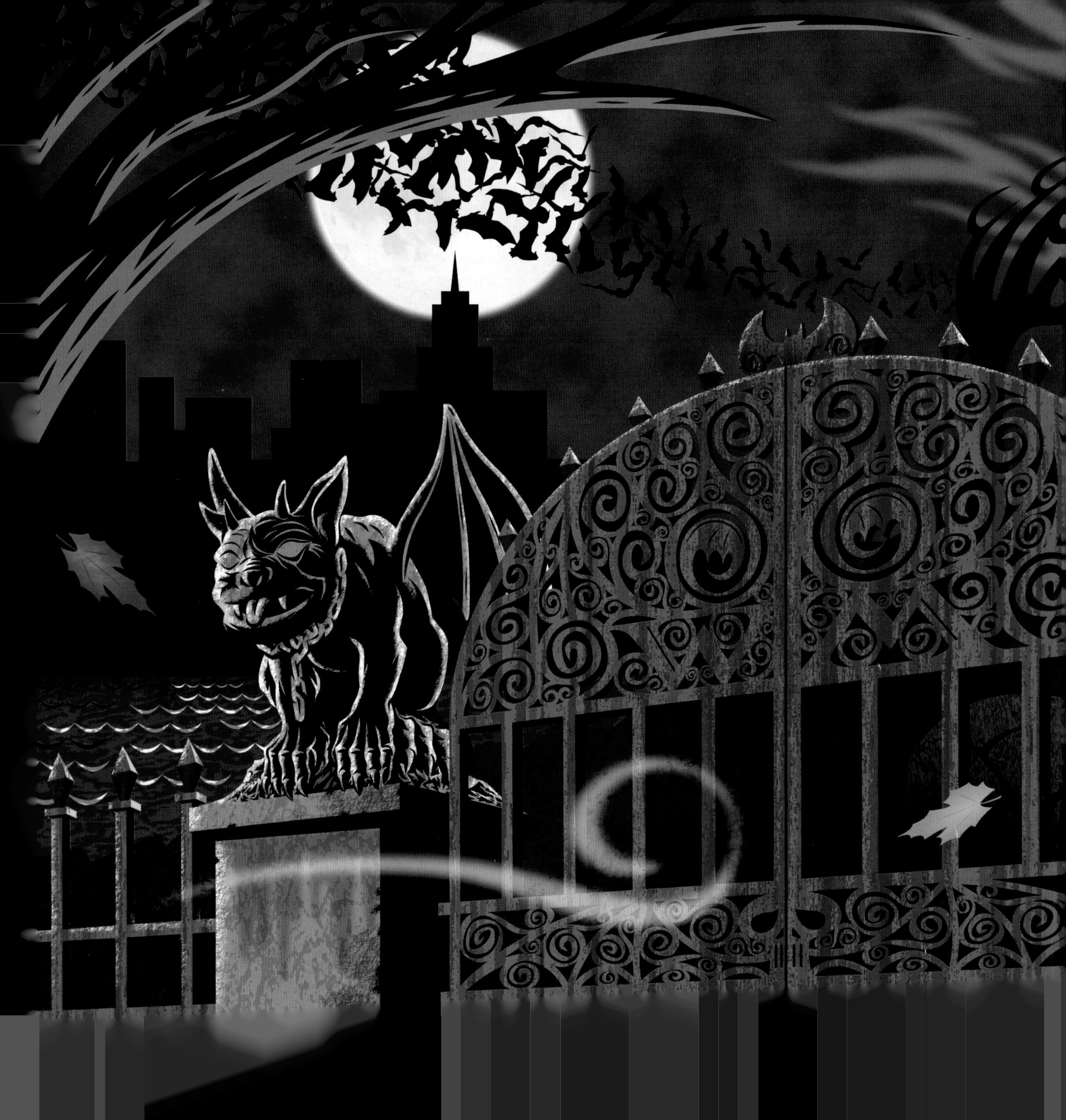

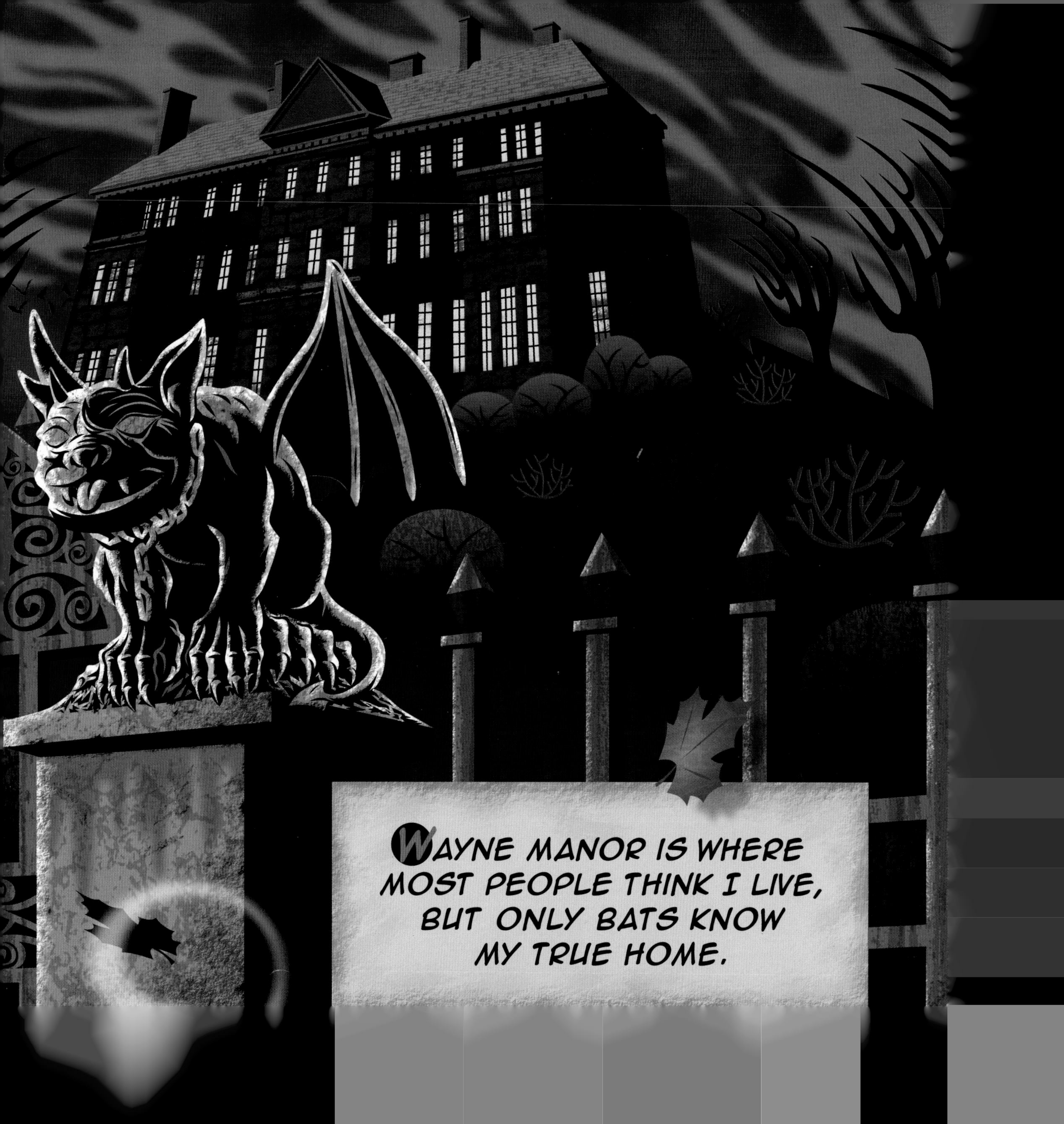

WAYNE MANOR IS WHERE MOST PEOPLE THINK I LIVE, BUT ONLY BATS KNOW MY TRUE HOME.

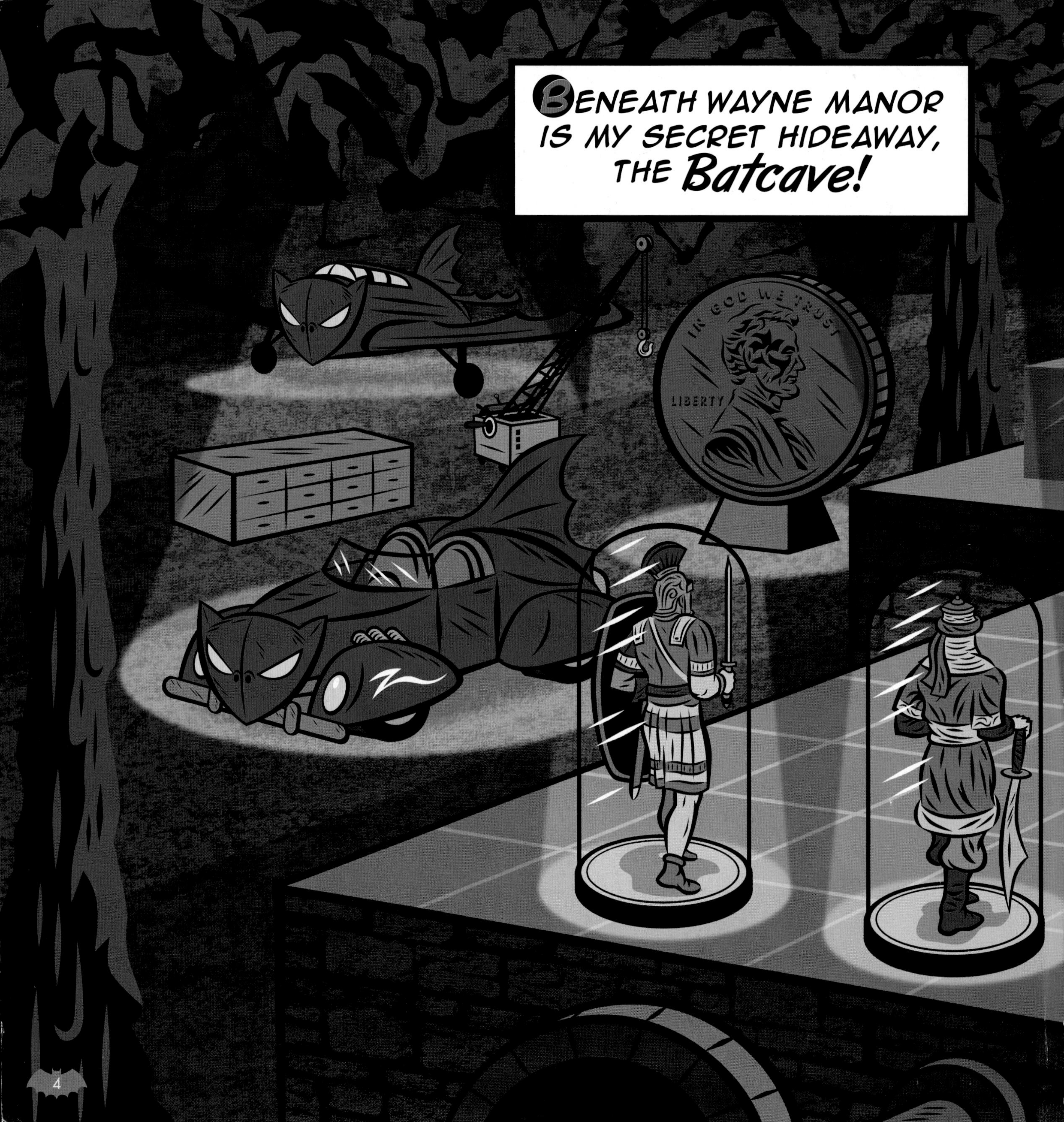
BENEATH WAYNE MANOR
IS MY SECRET HIDEAWAY,
THE Batcave!
IN GOD WE TRUST
LIBERTY

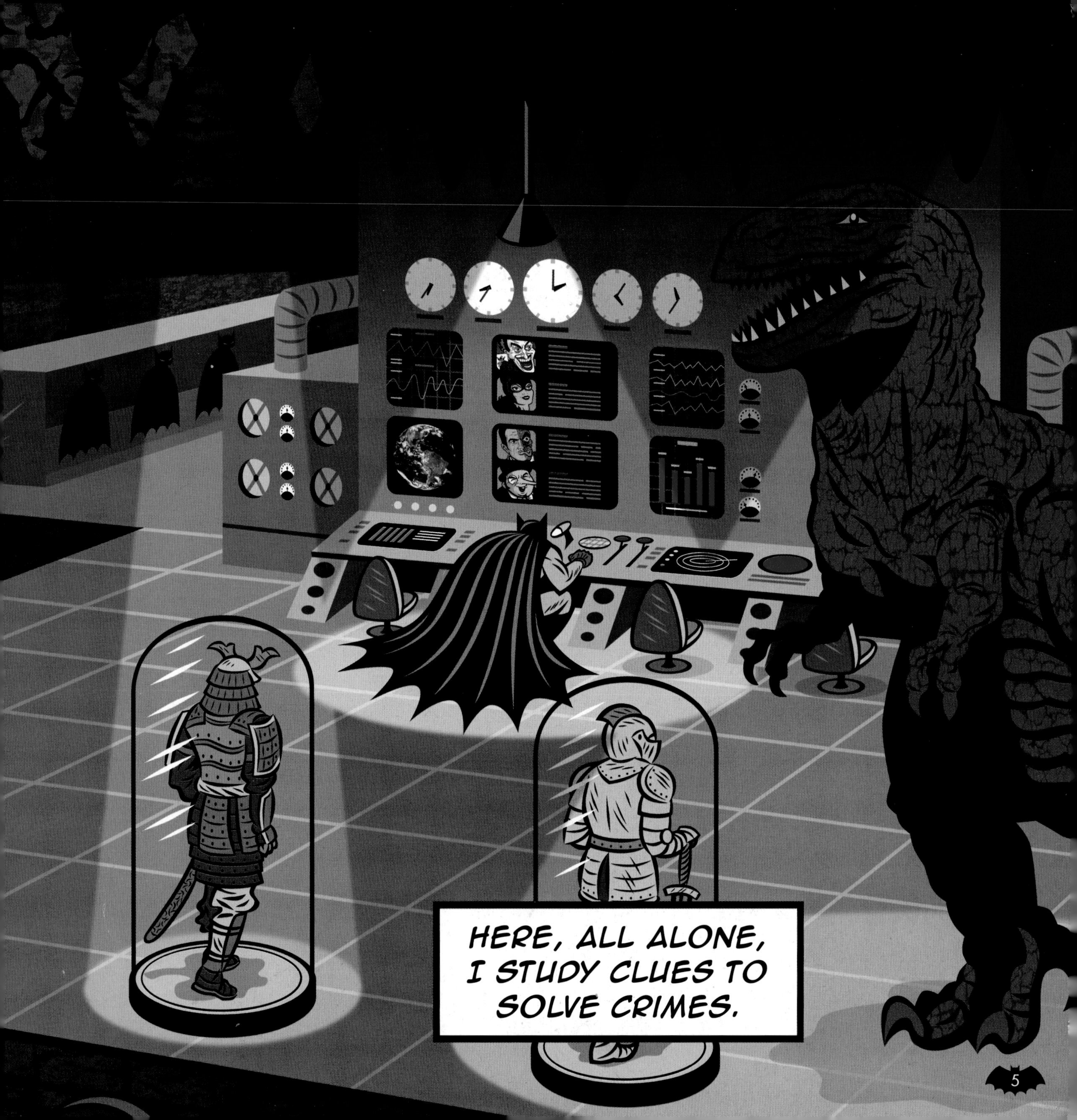
HERE, ALL ALONE,
I STUDY CLUES TO
SOLVE CRIMES.

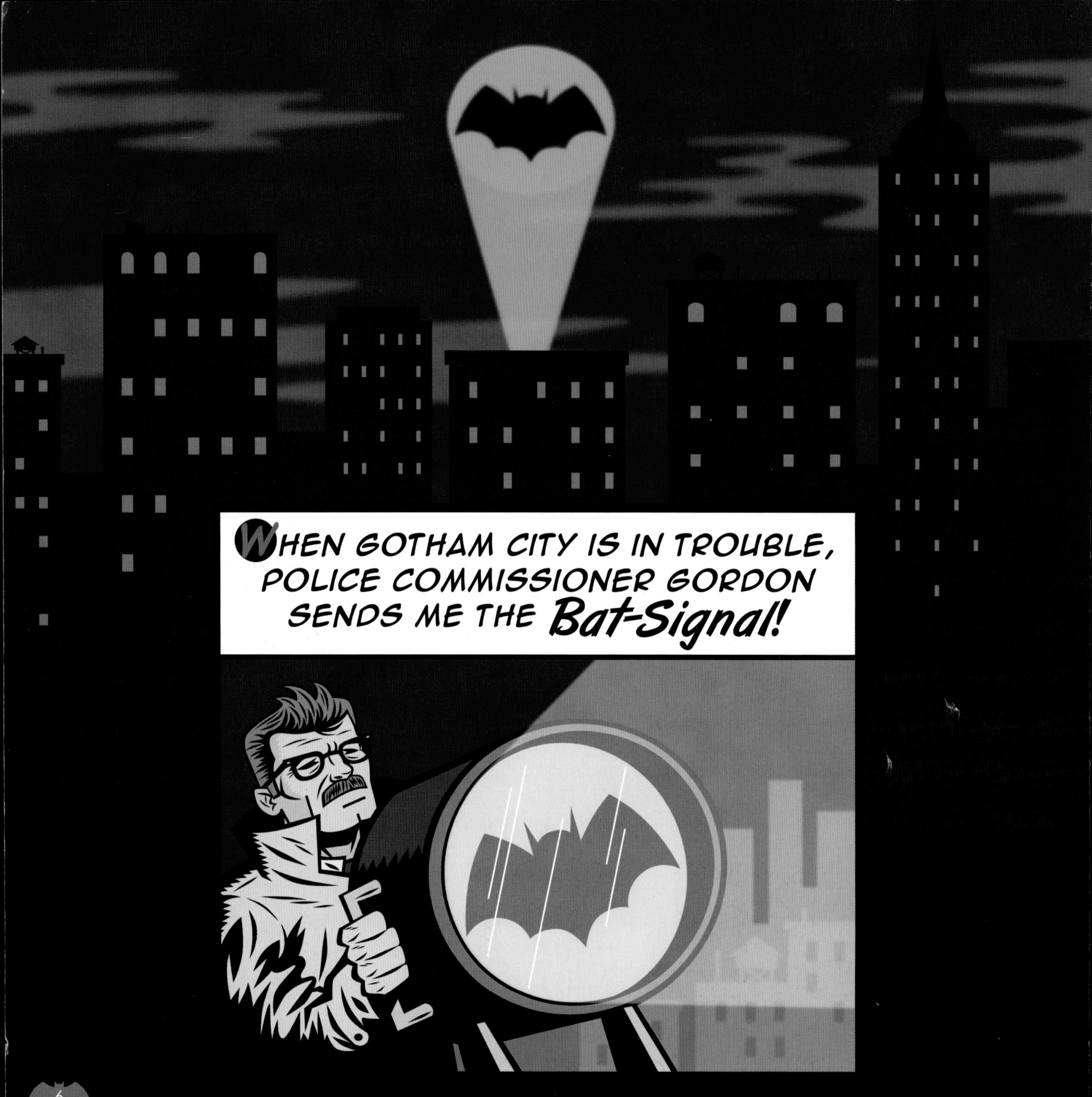
WHEN GOTHAM CITY IS IN TROUBLE,
POLICE COMMISSIONER GORDON
SENDS ME THE Bat-Signal!

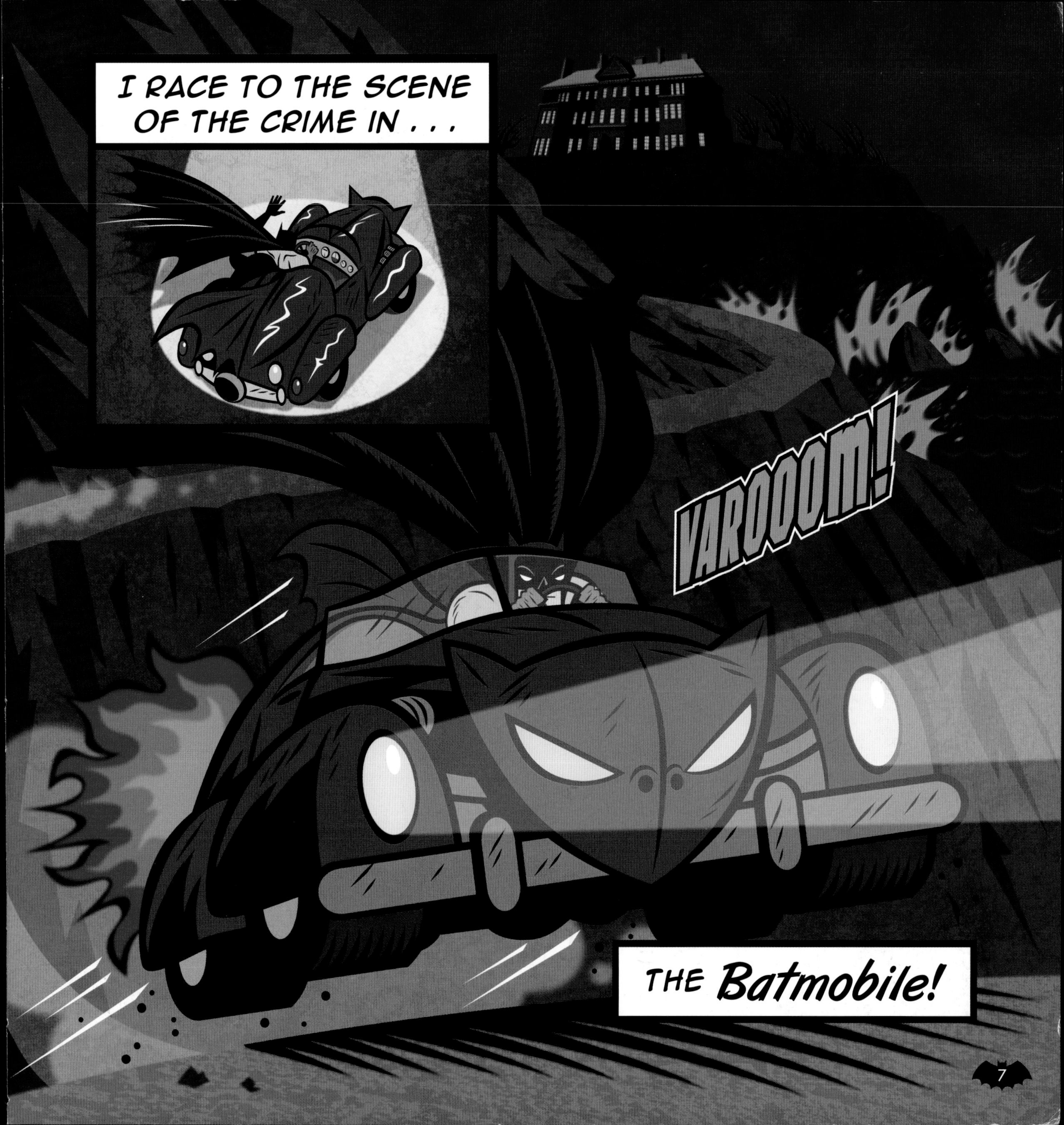
I RACE TO THE SCENE OF THE CRIME IN . . .
VAROOOM!
THE Batmobile!

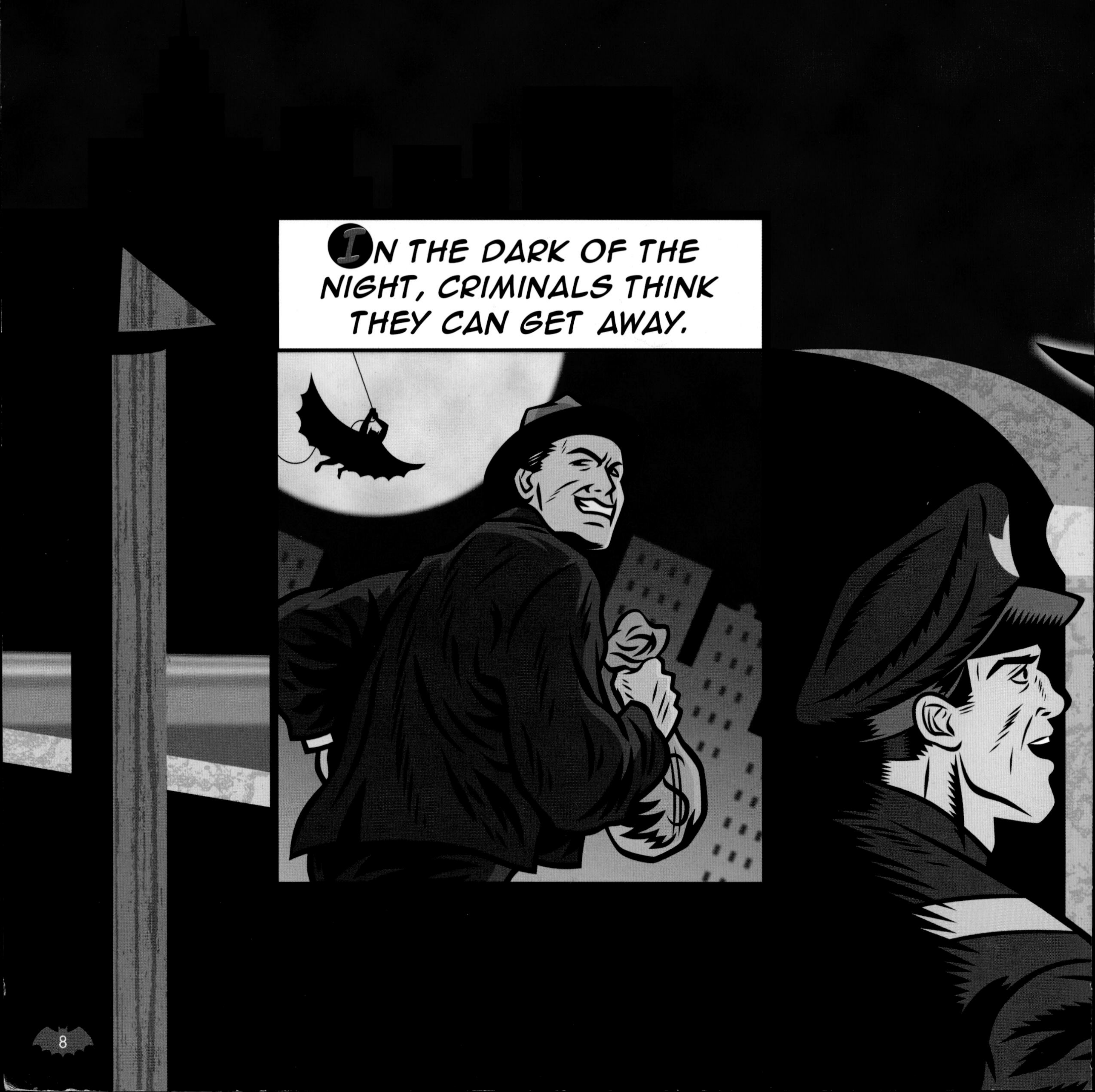
IN THE DARK OF THE NIGHT, CRIMINALS THINK THEY CAN GET AWAY.

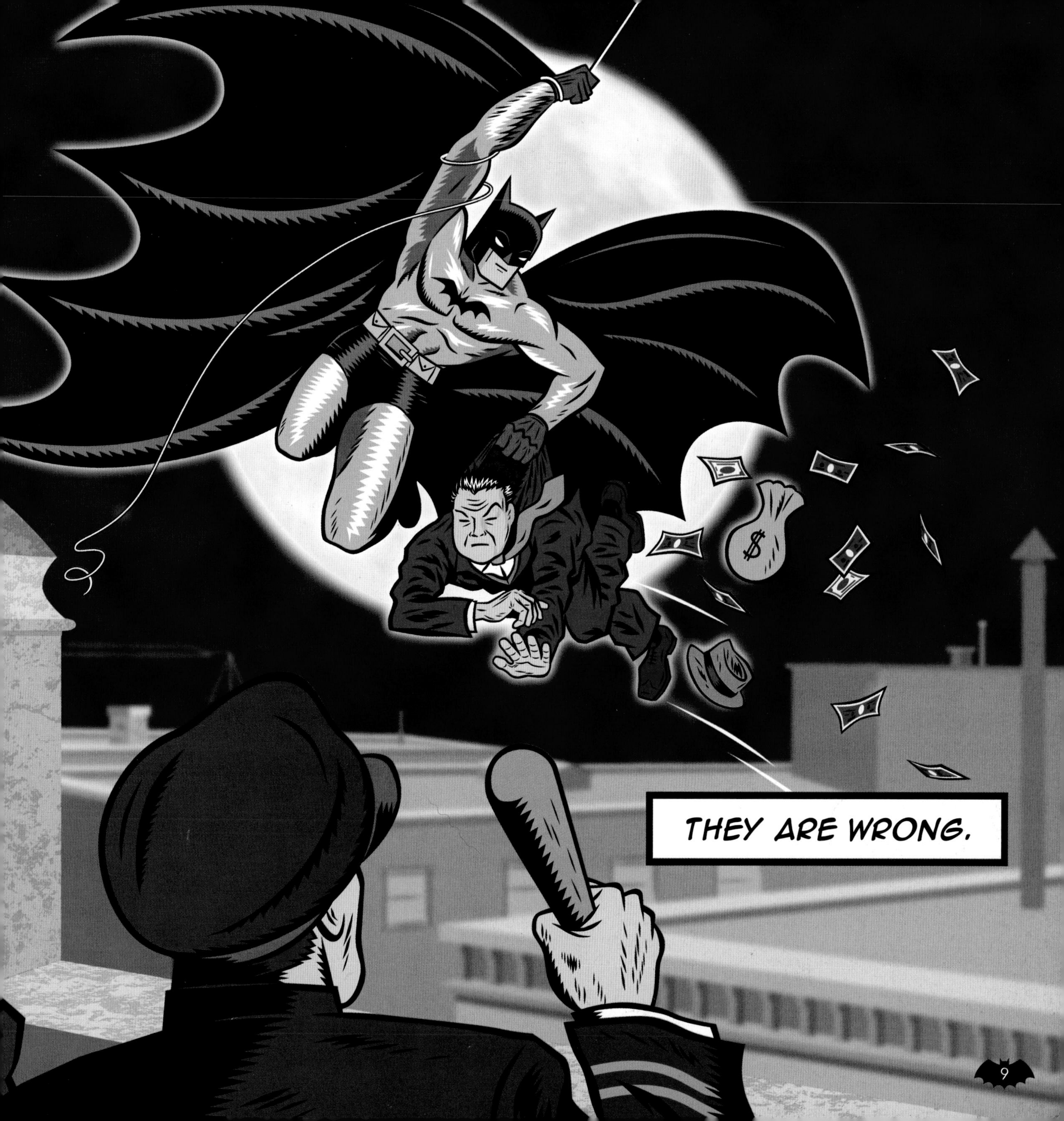
THEY ARE WRONG.

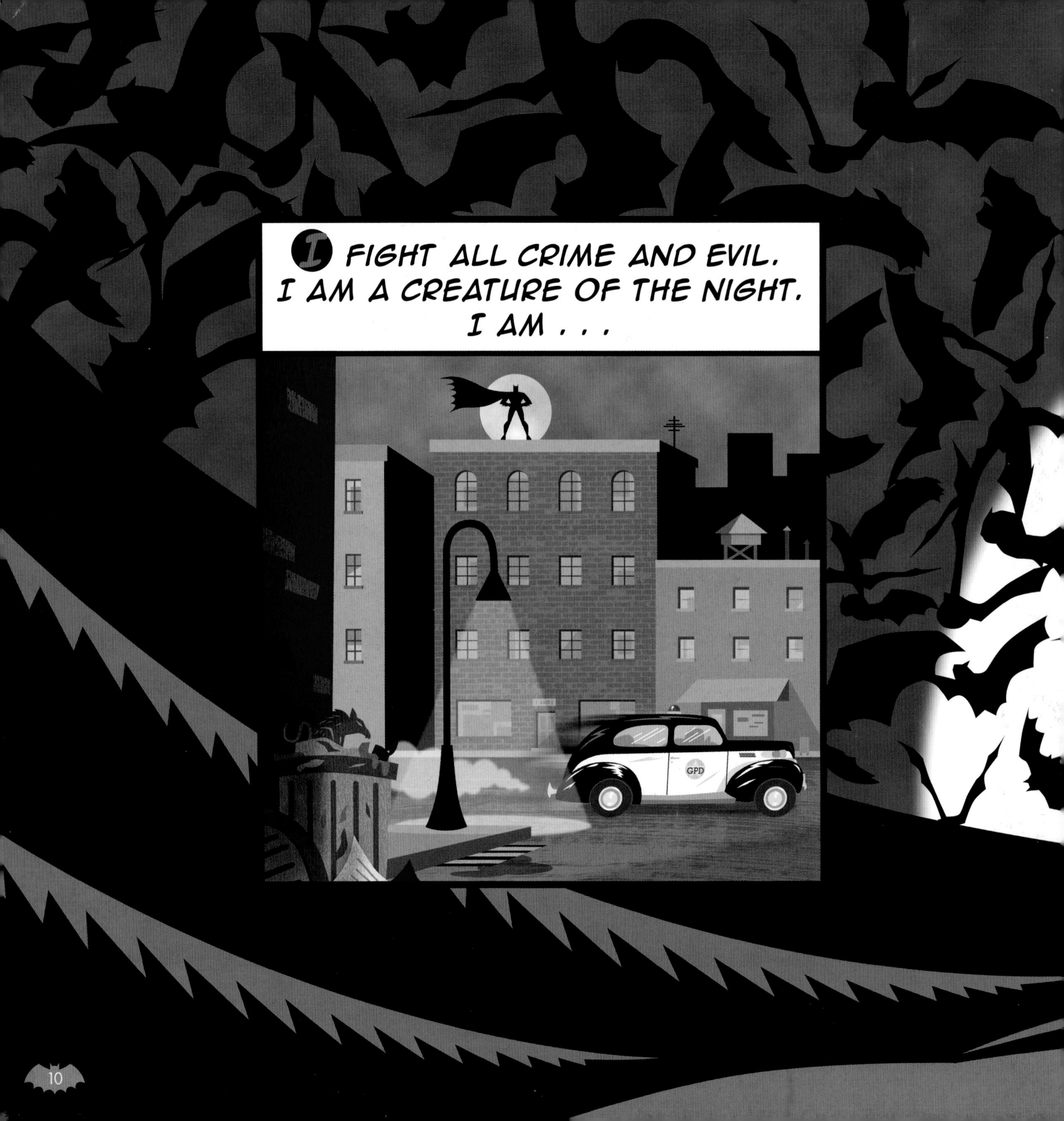
I FIGHT ALL CRIME AND EVIL.
I AM A CREATURE OF THE NIGHT.
I AM . . .
GPD

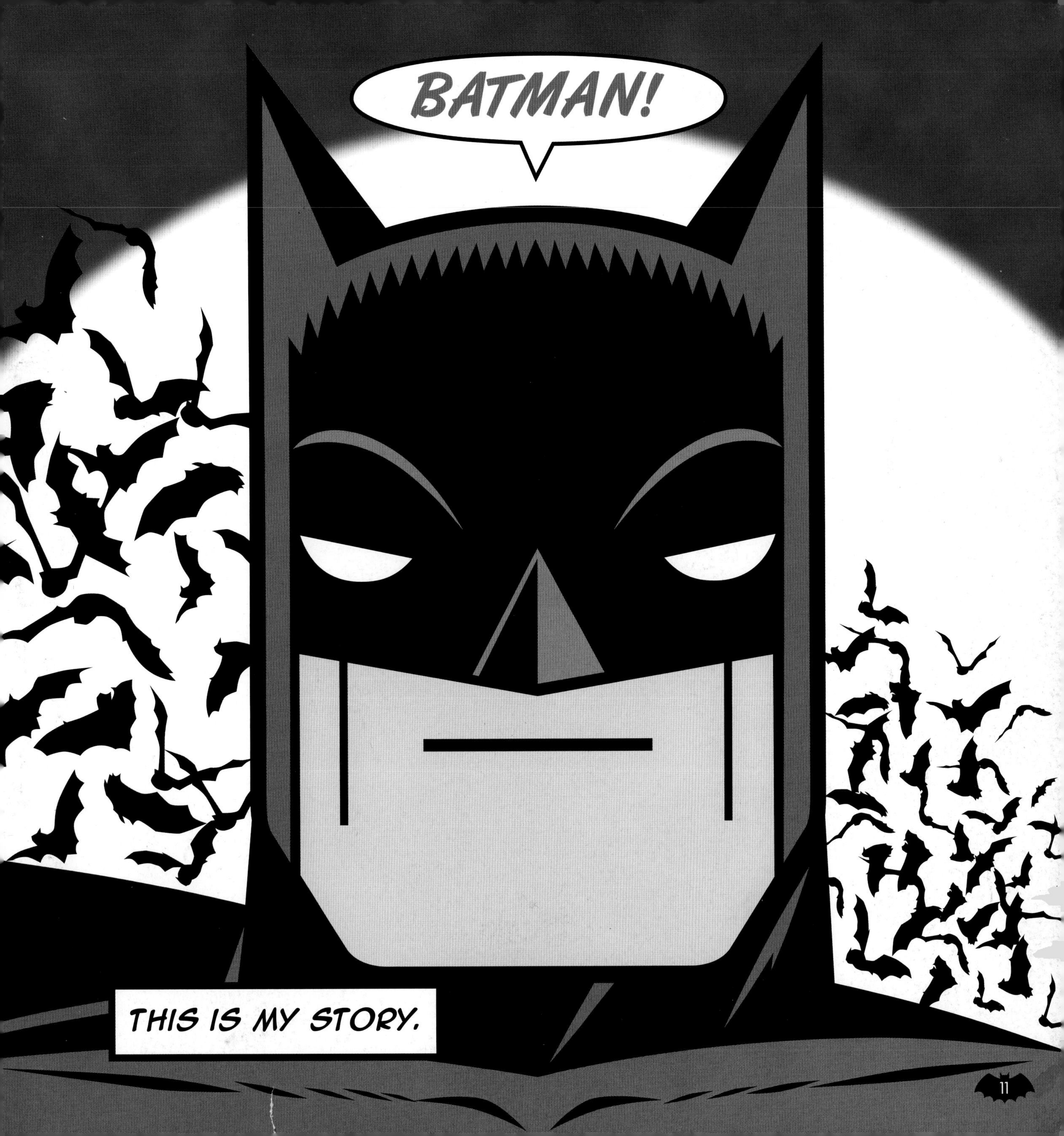
BATMAN!
THIS IS MY STORY.

MY REAL NAME IS BRUCE WAYNE. WHEN I WAS A BOY, MY PARENTS GAVE ME A LOT OF LOVE, AND I LOVED THEM, TOO.

WE ALWAYS HAD FUN TOGETHER, ESPECIALLY WHEN I PRETENDED TO BE MY FAVORITE HERO.

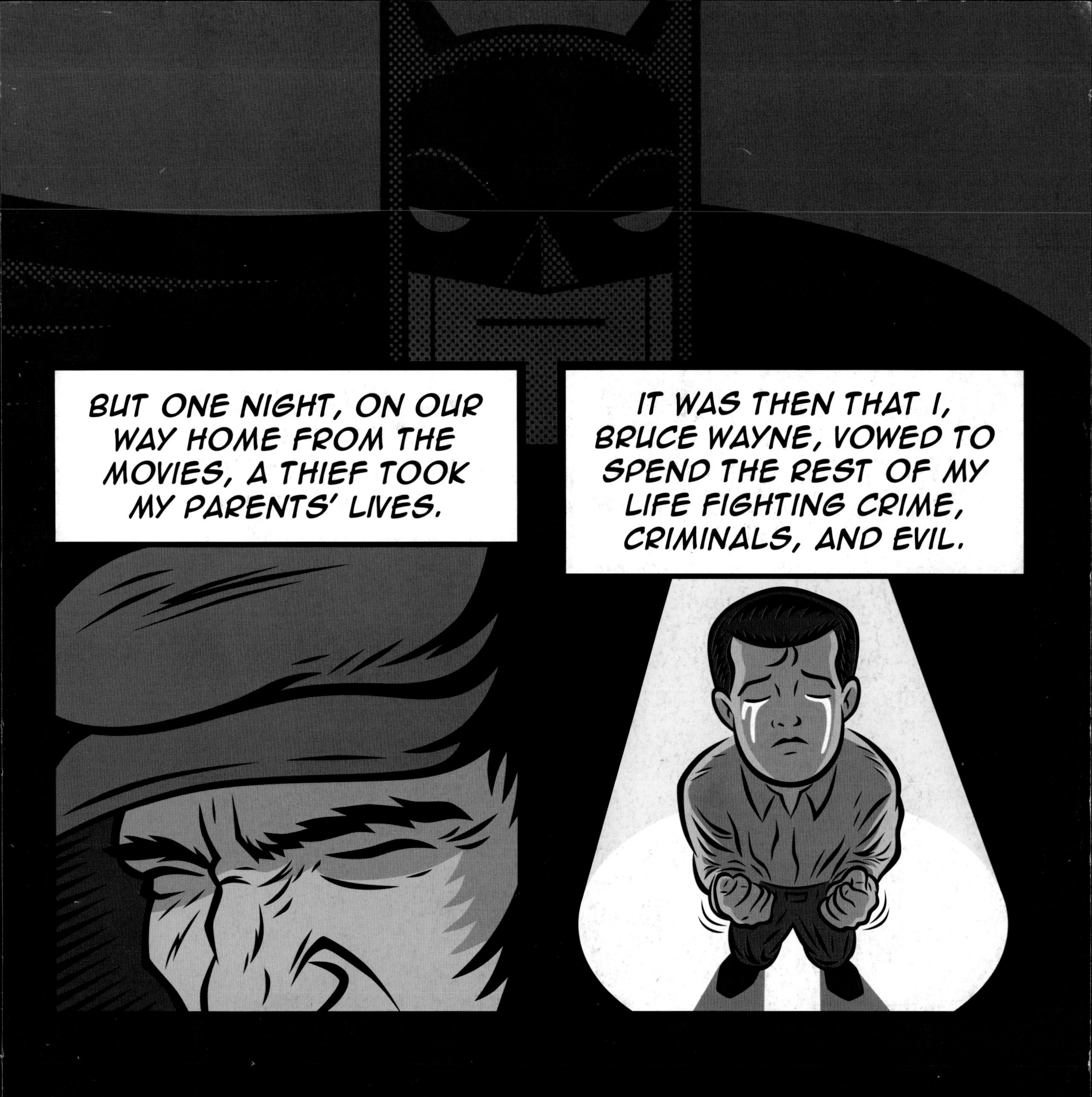
BUT ONE NIGHT, ON OUR WAY HOME FROM THE MOVIES, A THIEF TOOK MY PARENTS' LIVES.
IT WAS THEN THAT I, BRUCE WAYNE, VOWED TO SPEND THE REST OF MY LIFE FIGHTING CRIME, CRIMINALS, AND EVIL.

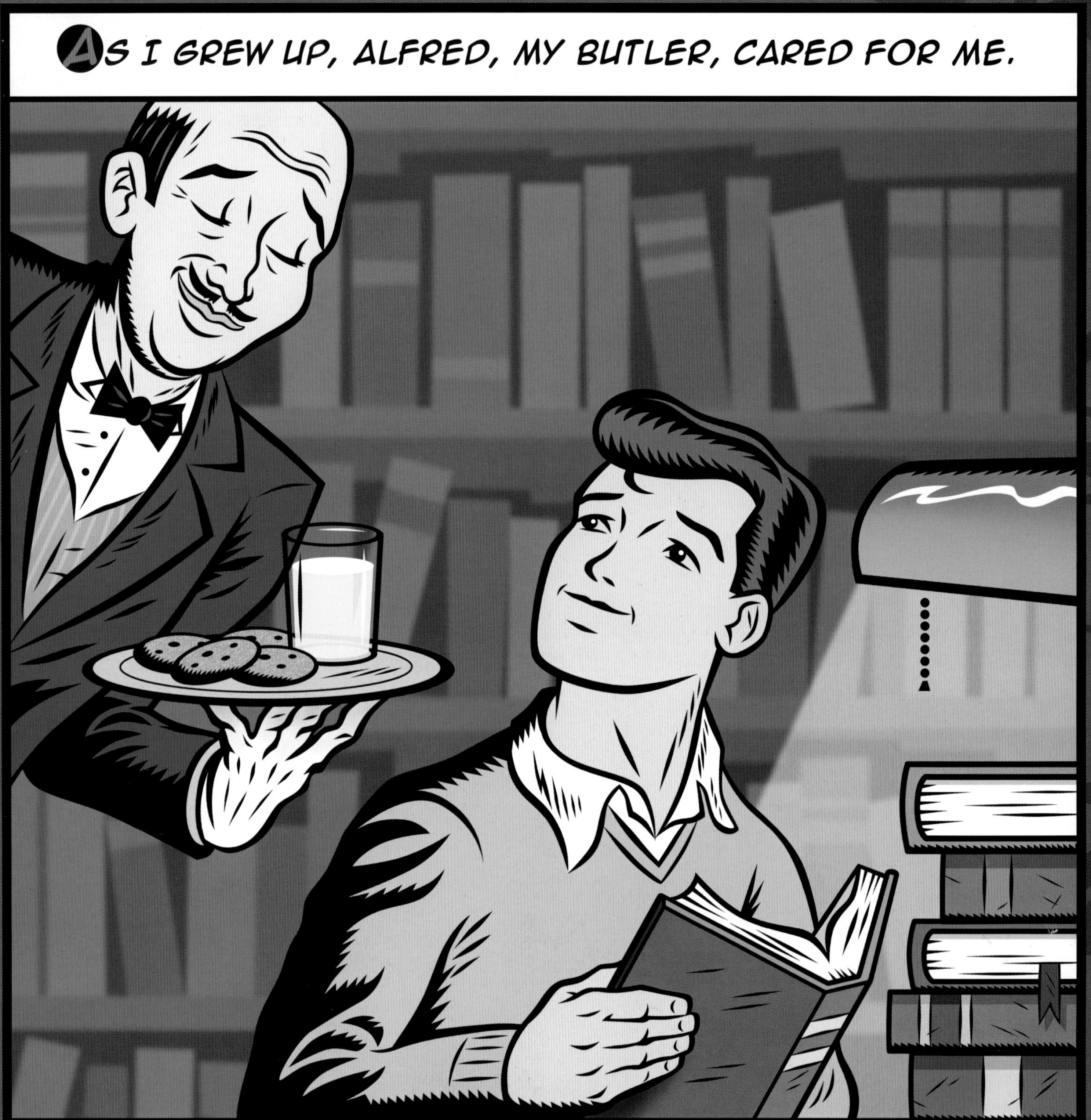
AS I GREW UP, ALFRED, MY BUTLER, CARED FOR ME.

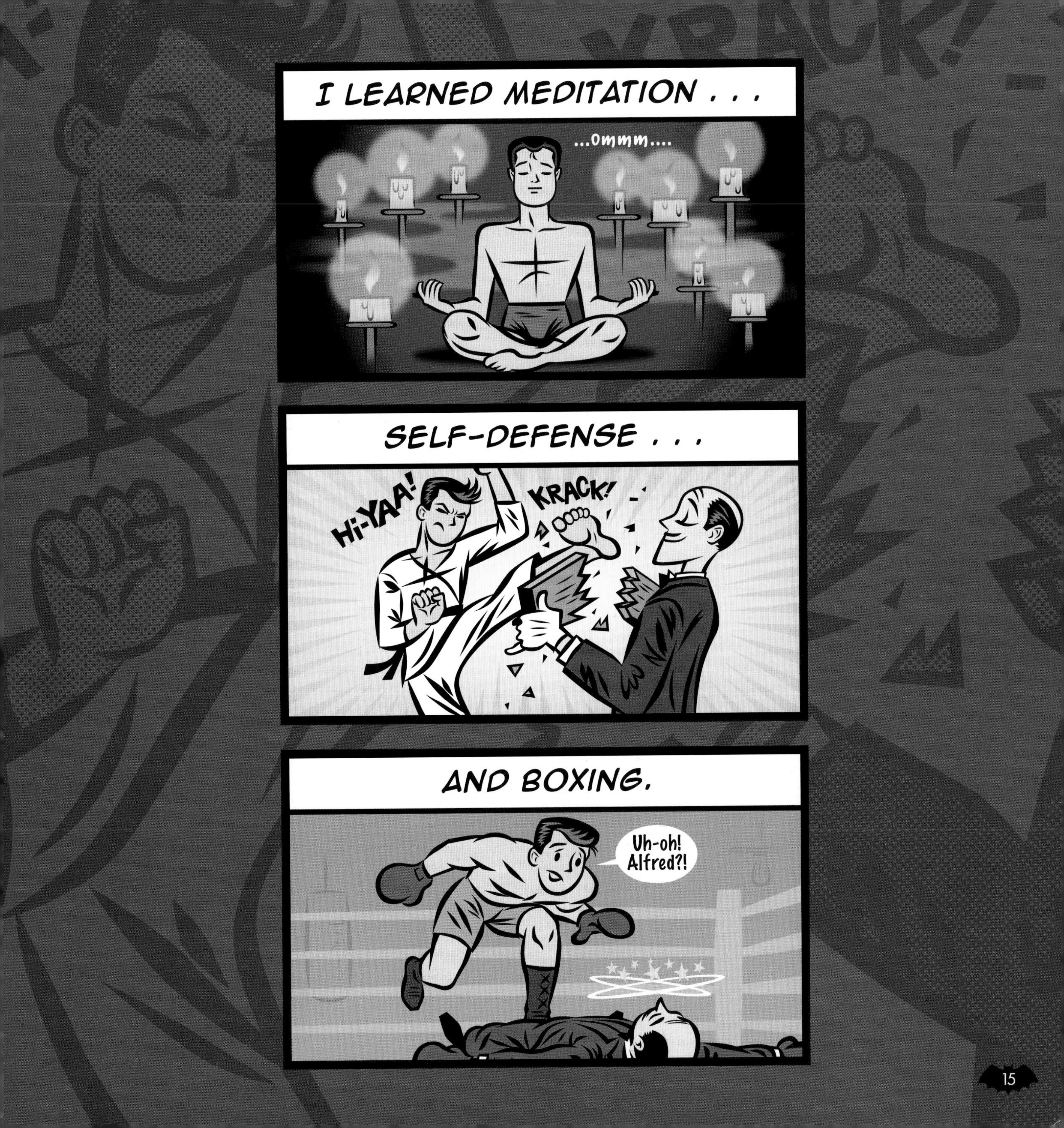
I LEARNED MEDITATION . . .
...ommm....
SELF-DEFENSE . . .
HI-YAA!
KRACK!
AND BOXING.
Uh-oh! Alfred?!

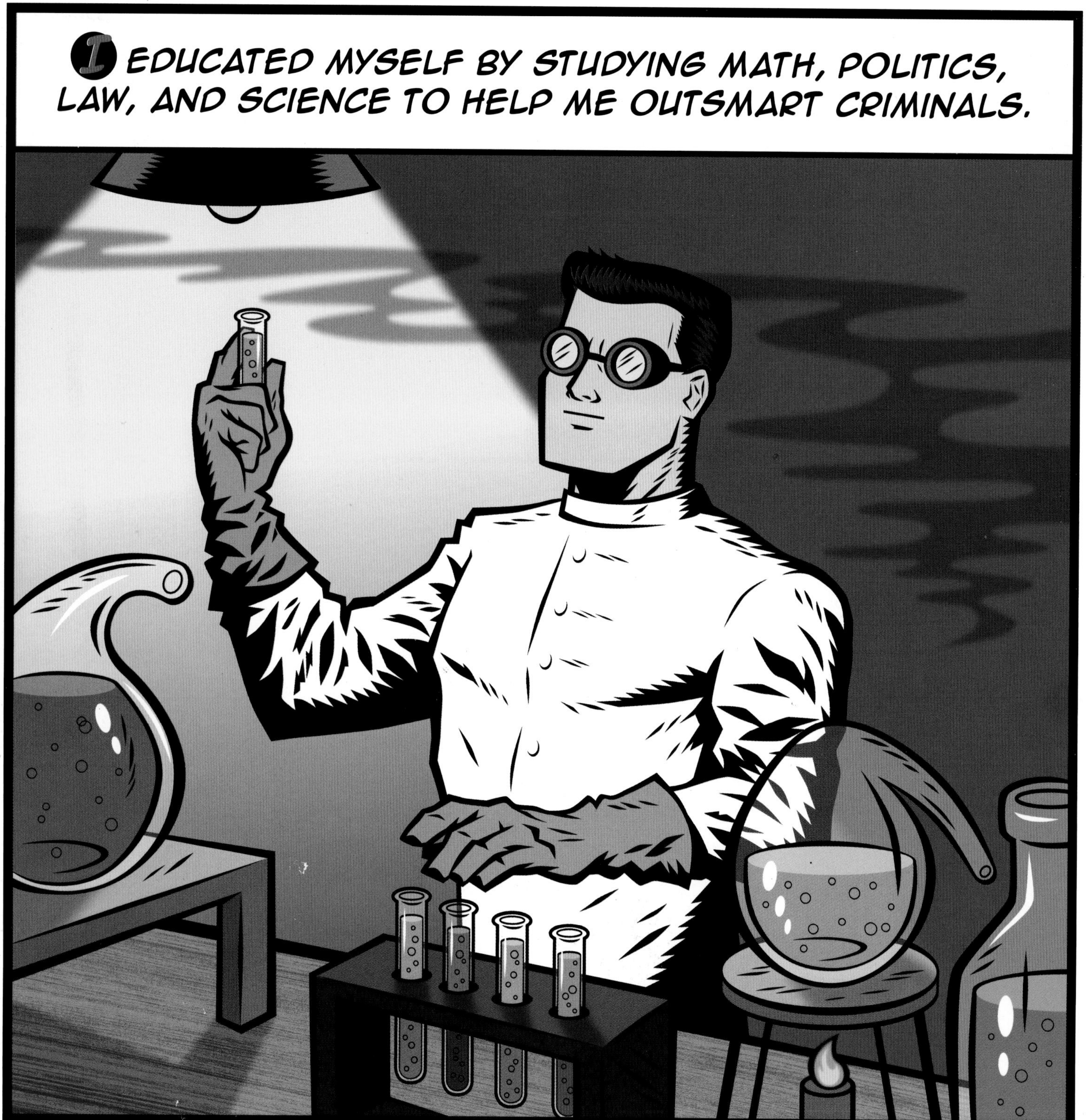
I EDUCATED MYSELF BY STUDYING MATH, POLITICS, LAW, AND SCIENCE TO HELP ME OUTSMART CRIMINALS.

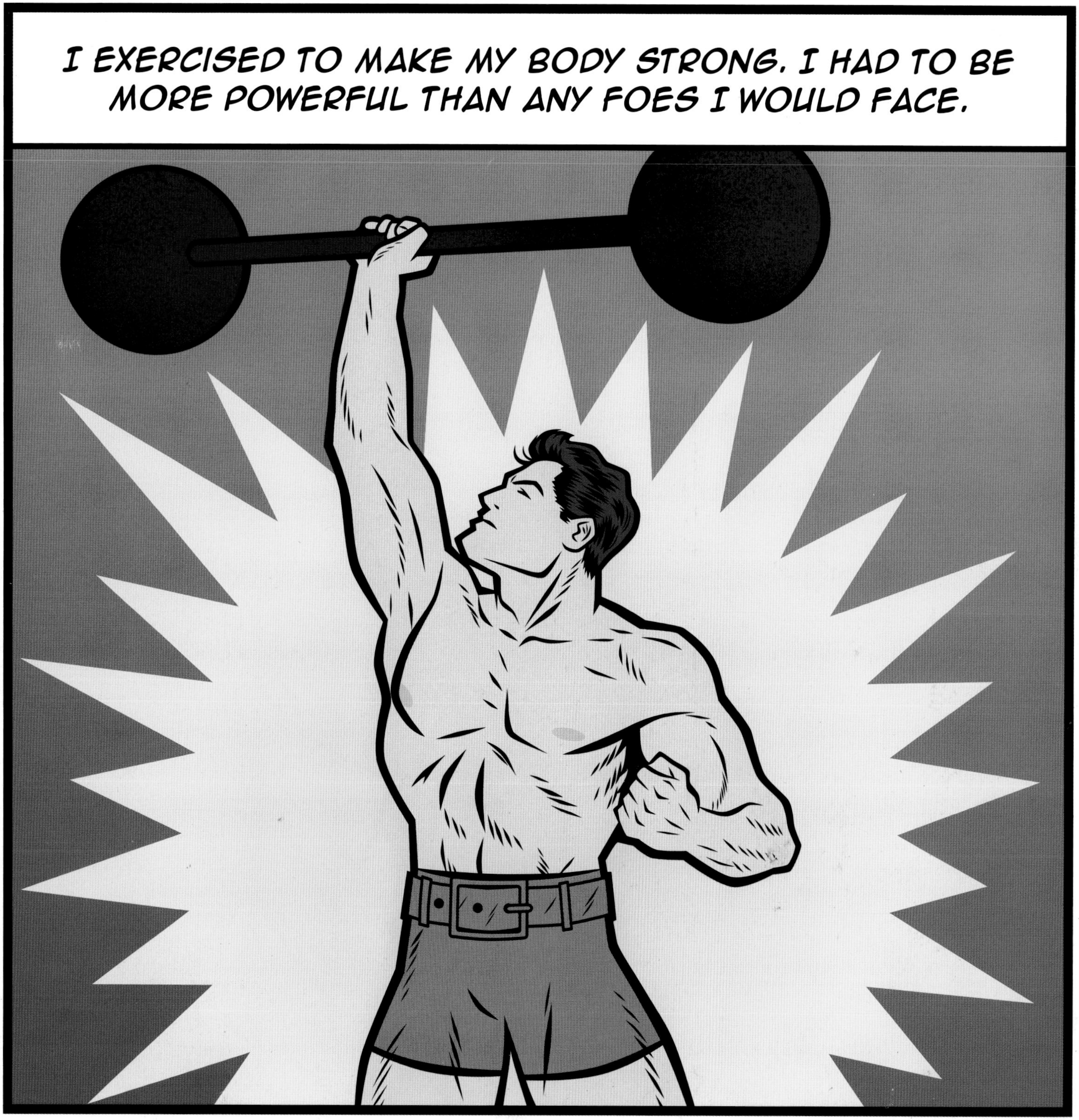
I EXERCISED TO MAKE MY BODY STRONG. I HAD TO BE MORE POWERFUL THAN ANY FOES I WOULD FACE.

ONE NIGHT, A BAT FLEW PAST MY WINDOW AND GAVE ME A BRILLIANT IDEA. TO FRIGHTEN VILLAINS, I BECAME . . .

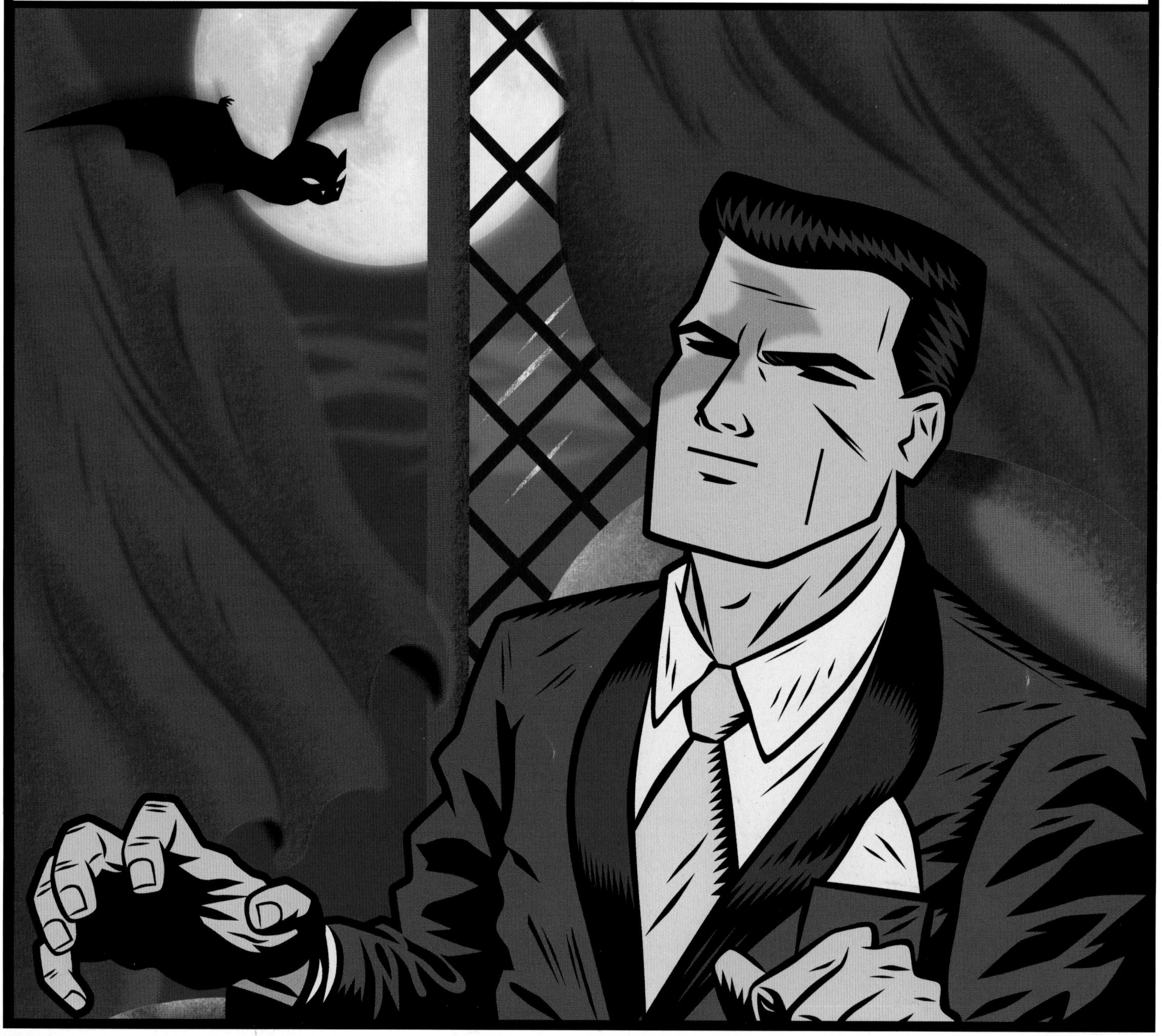

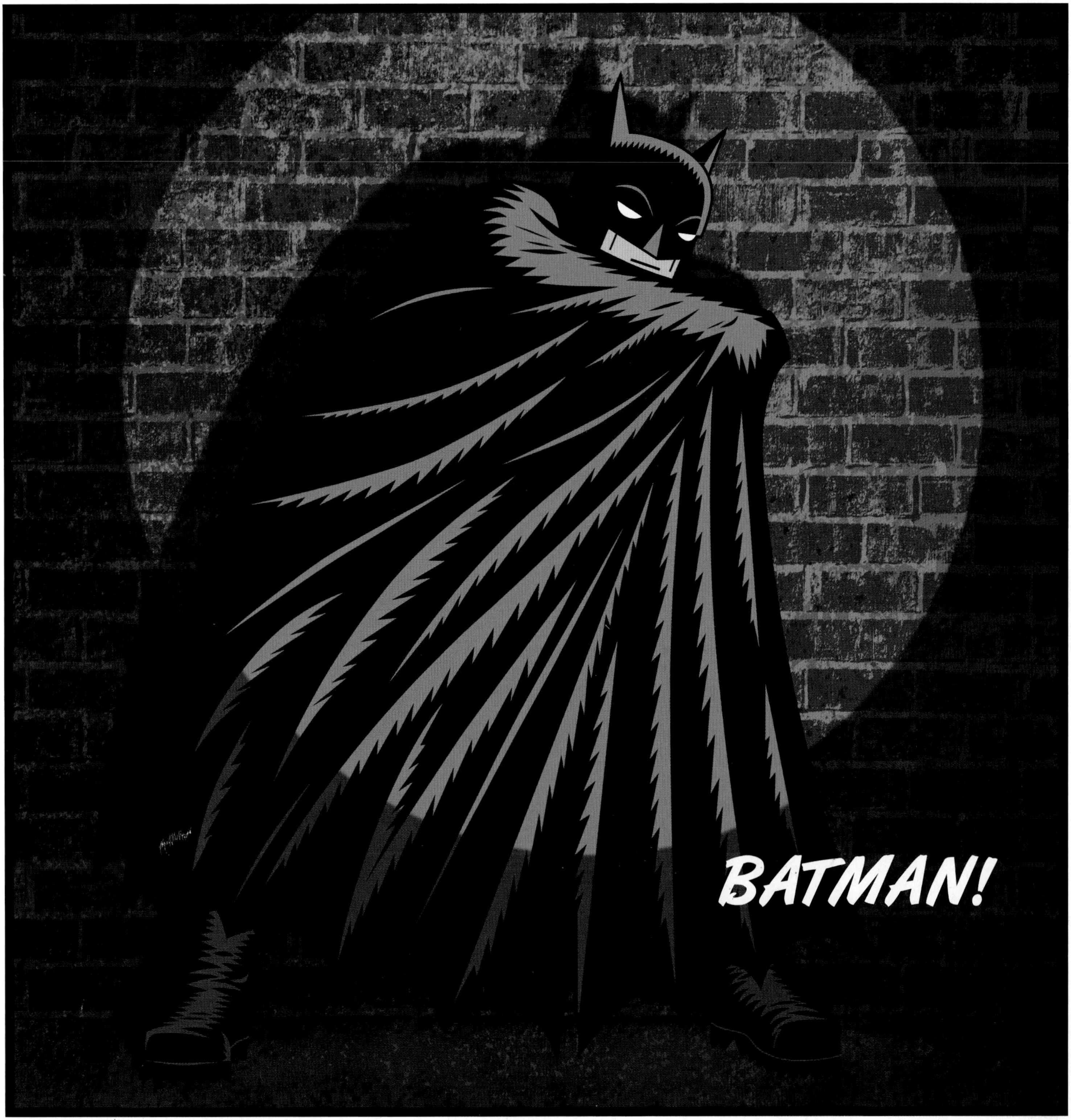
BATMAN!

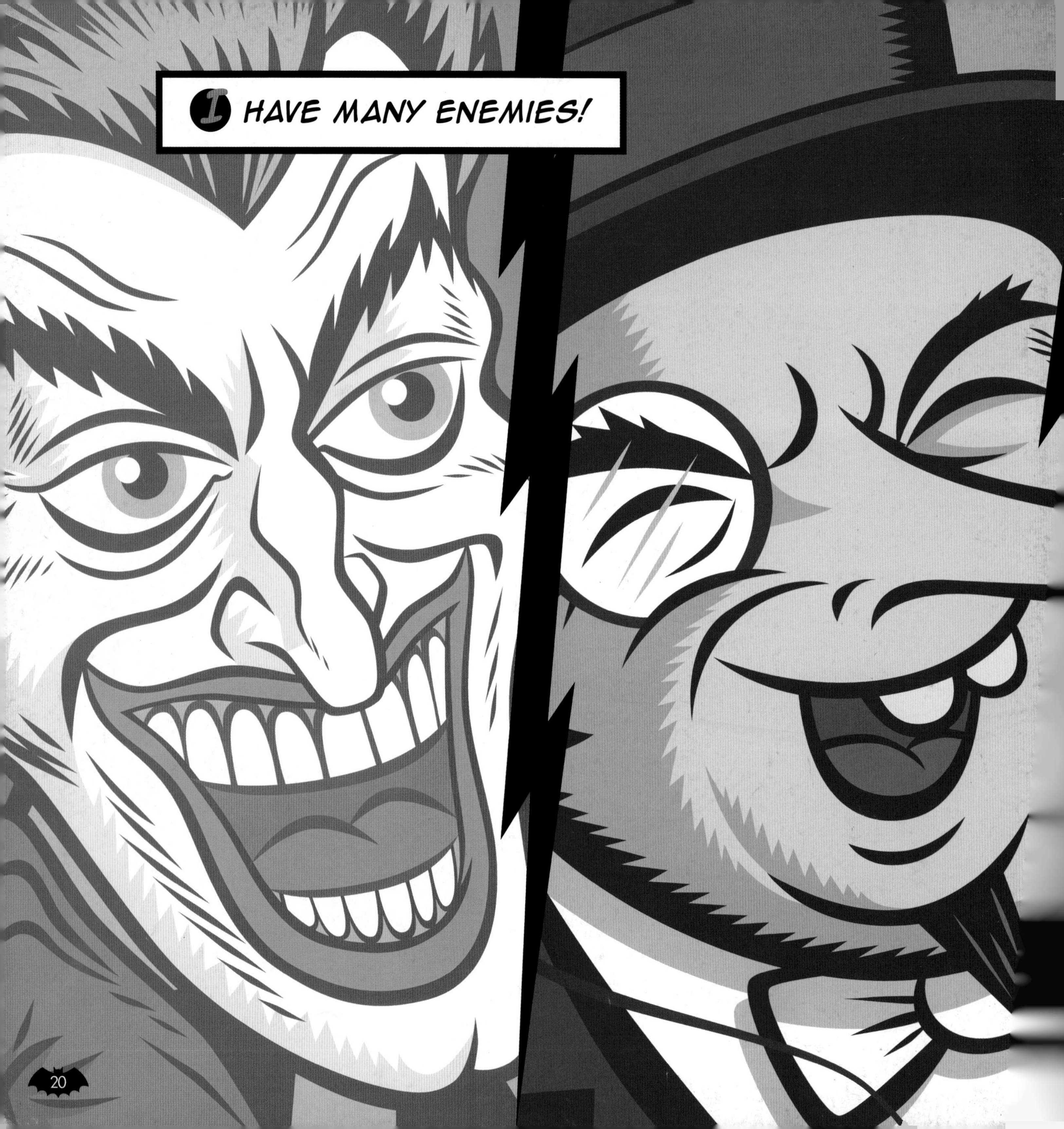
I HAVE MANY ENEMIES!

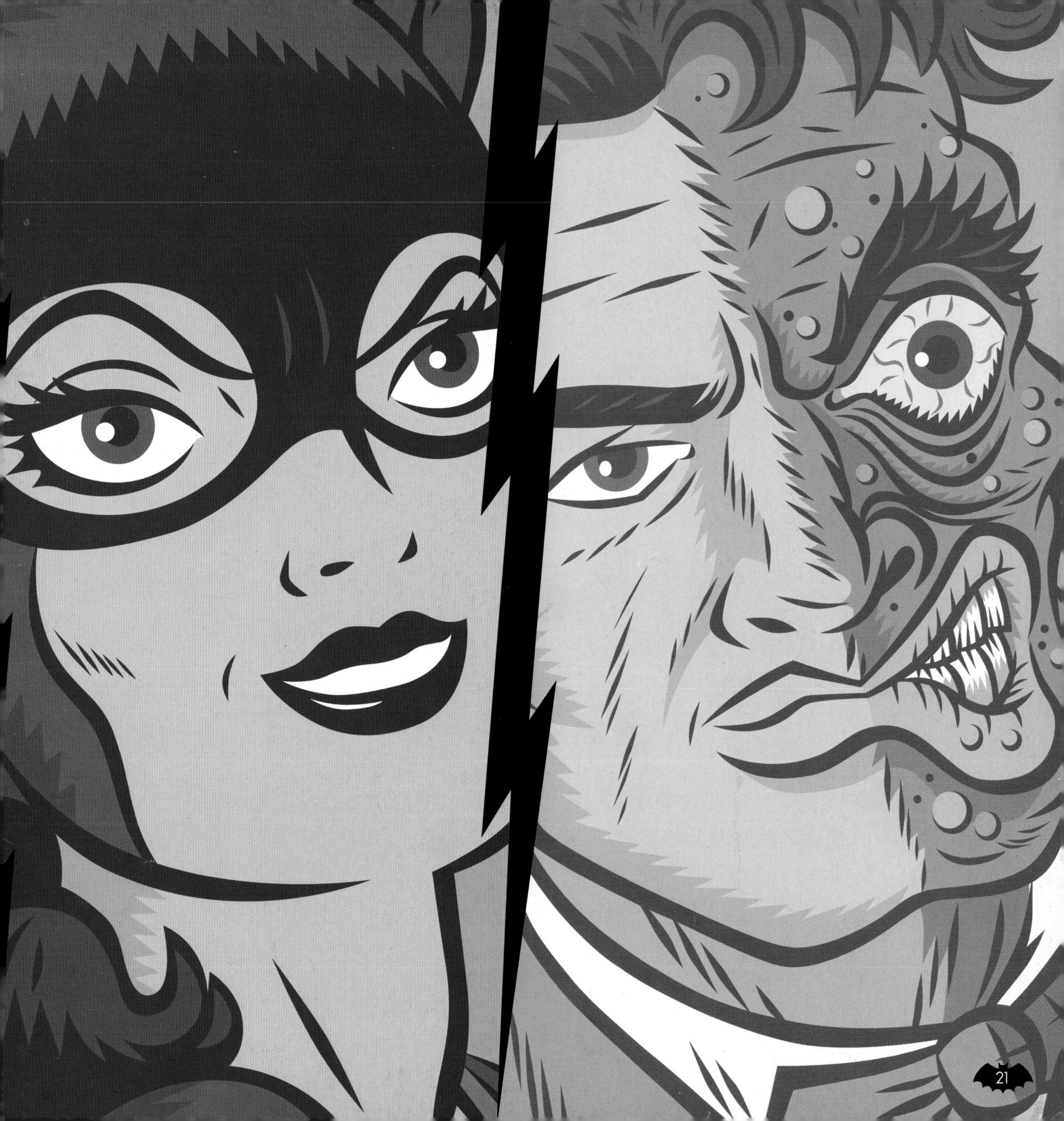

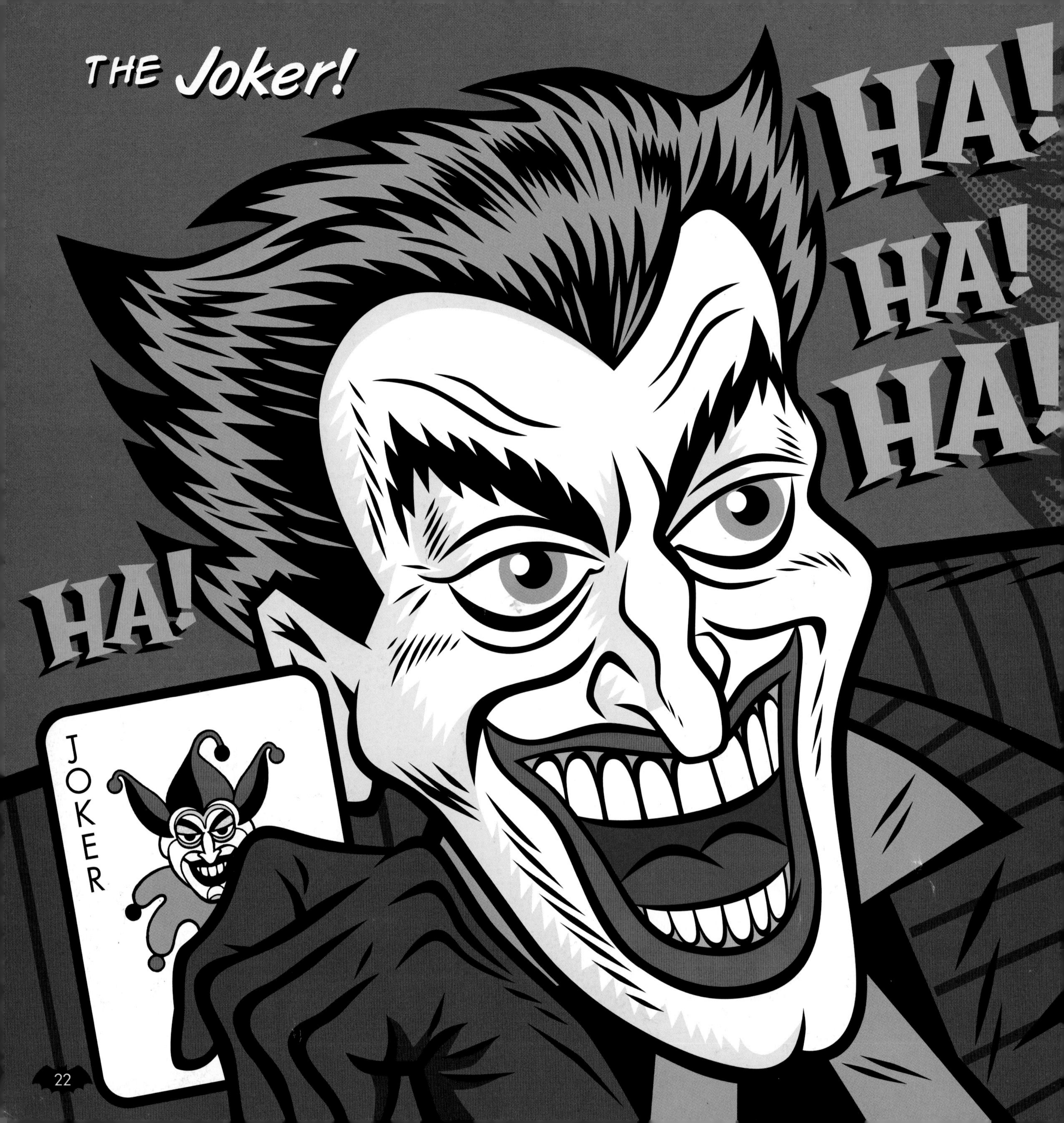
THE Joker!
HA!
HA!
HA!
HA!
JOKER

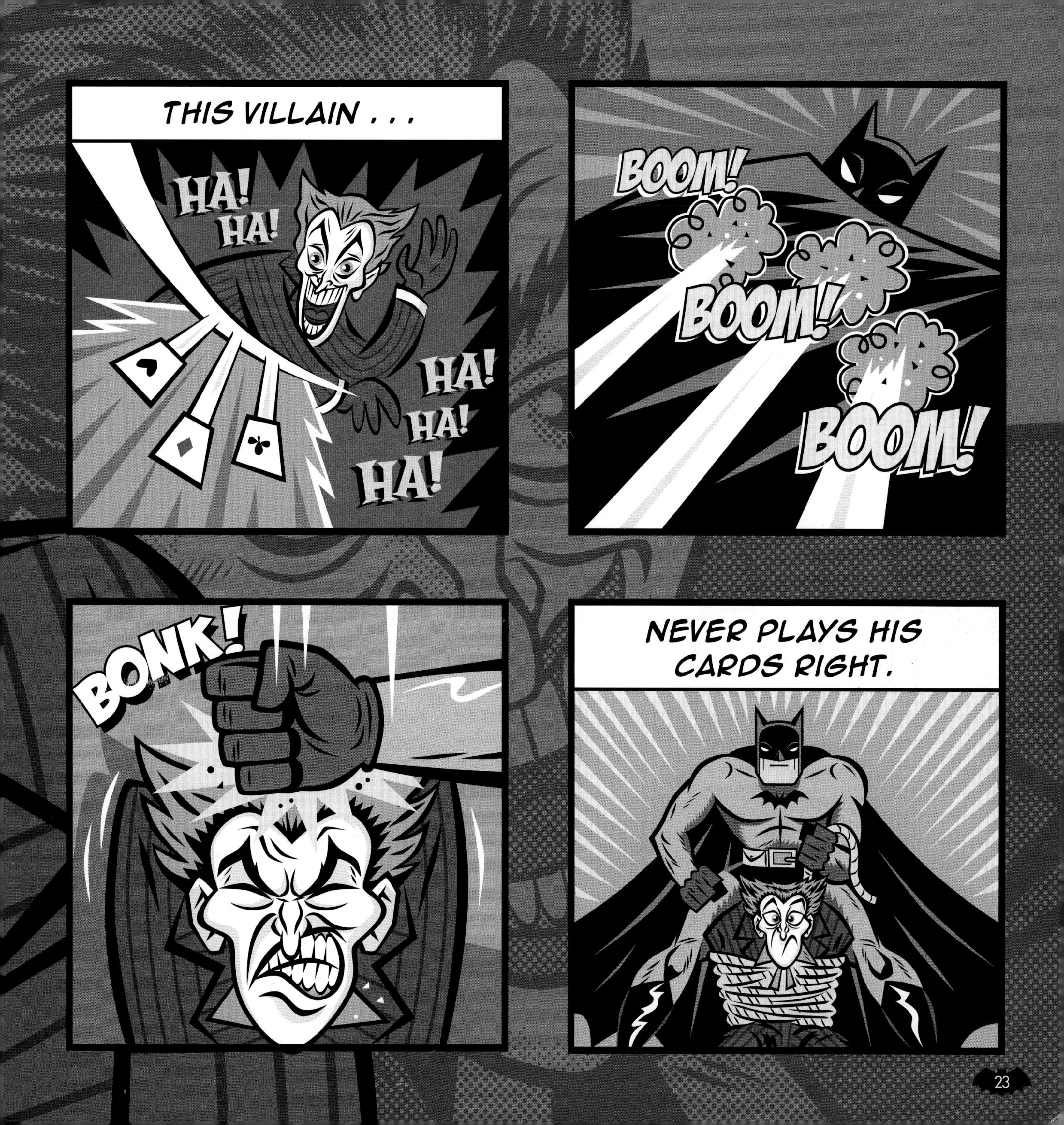
THIS VILLAIN . . .
HA!
HA!
HA!
HA!
HA!
BOOM!
BOOM!
BOOM!
BONK!
NEVER PLAYS HIS
CARDS RIGHT.

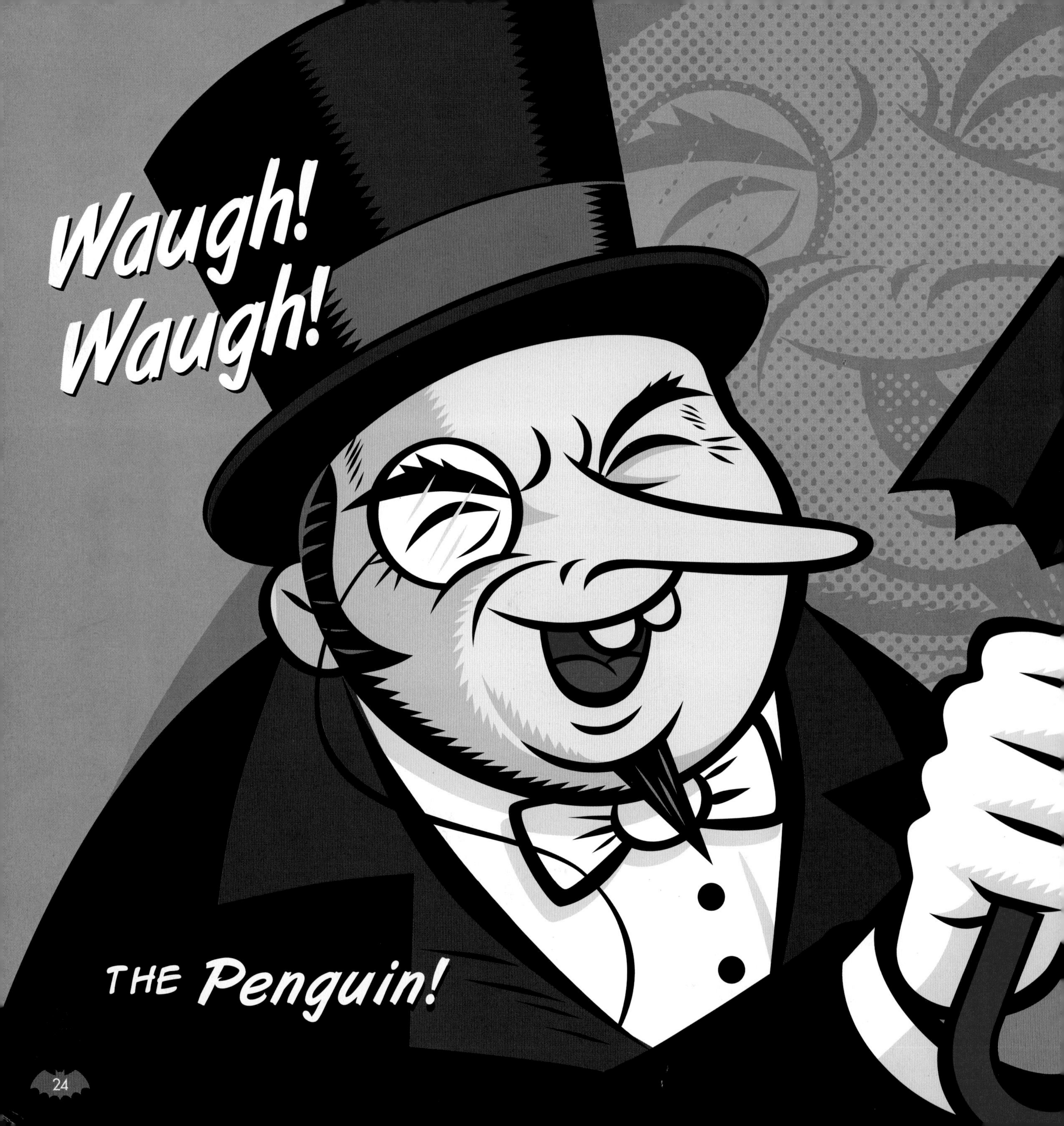
Waugh! Waugh!
THE Penguin!

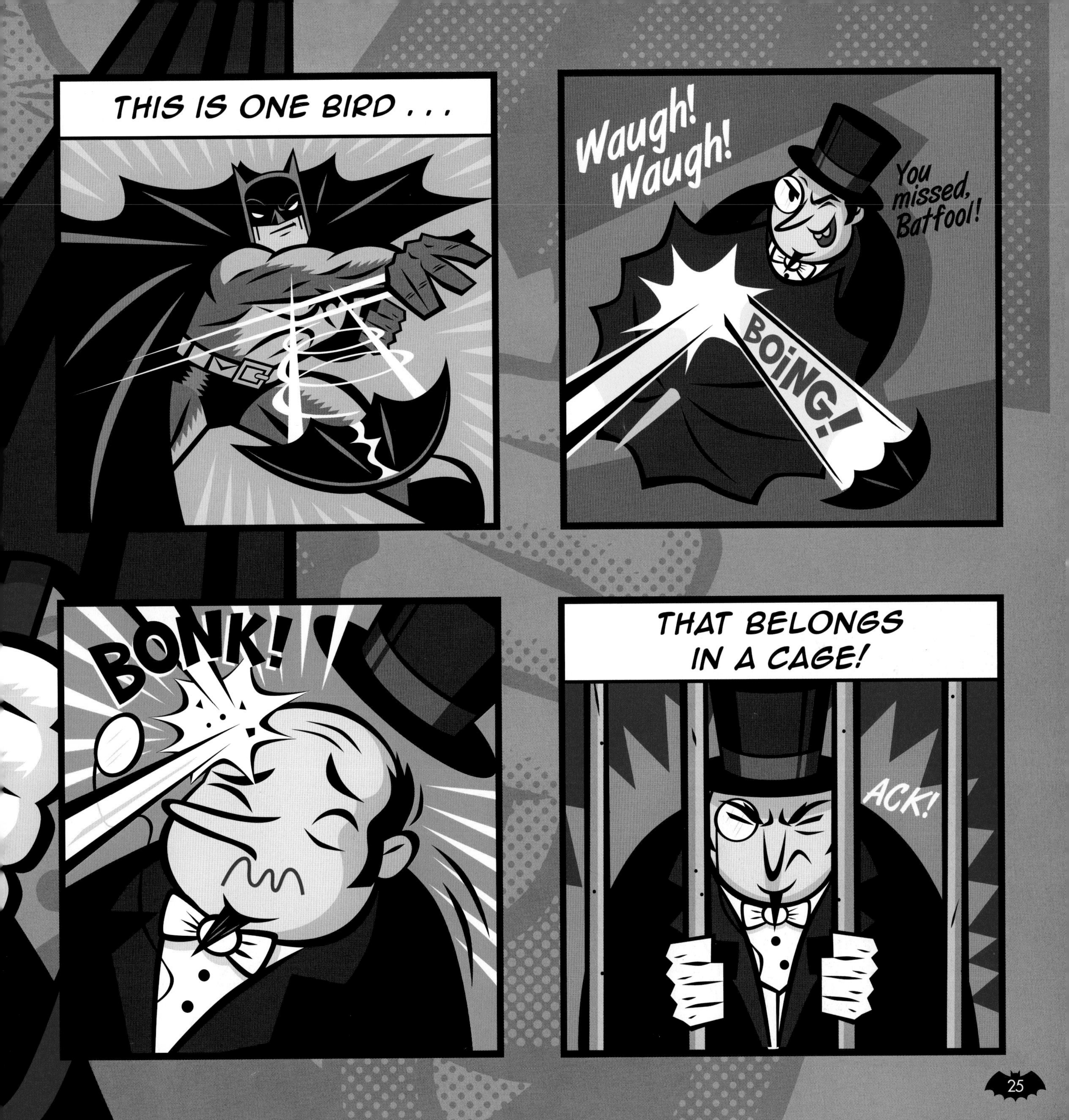

THIS IS ONE BIRD . . .
Waugh! Waugh!
You missed, Batfool!
BOING!
BONK!
THAT BELONGS IN A CAGE!
ACK!

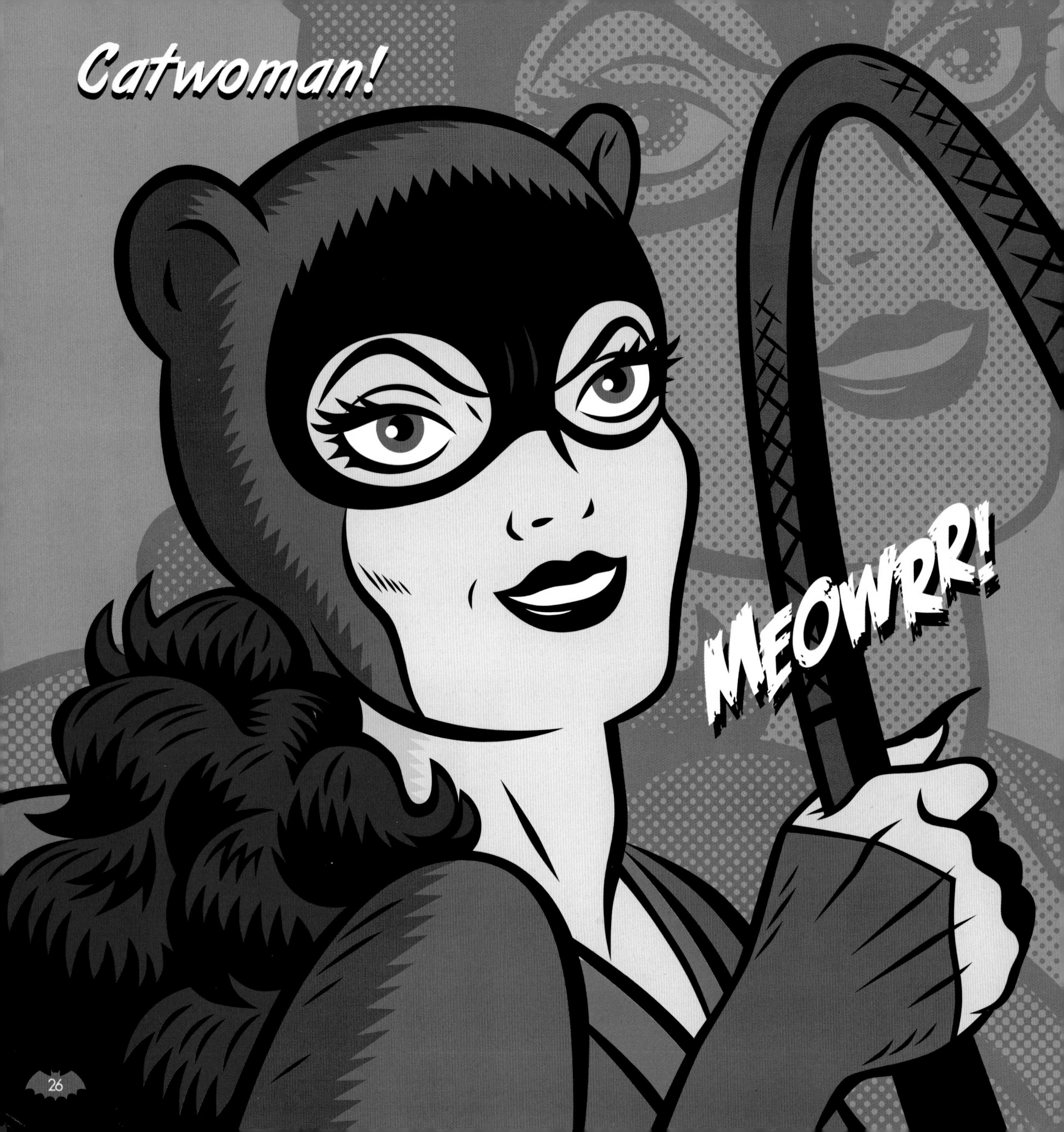
Catwoman!
MEOWRR!

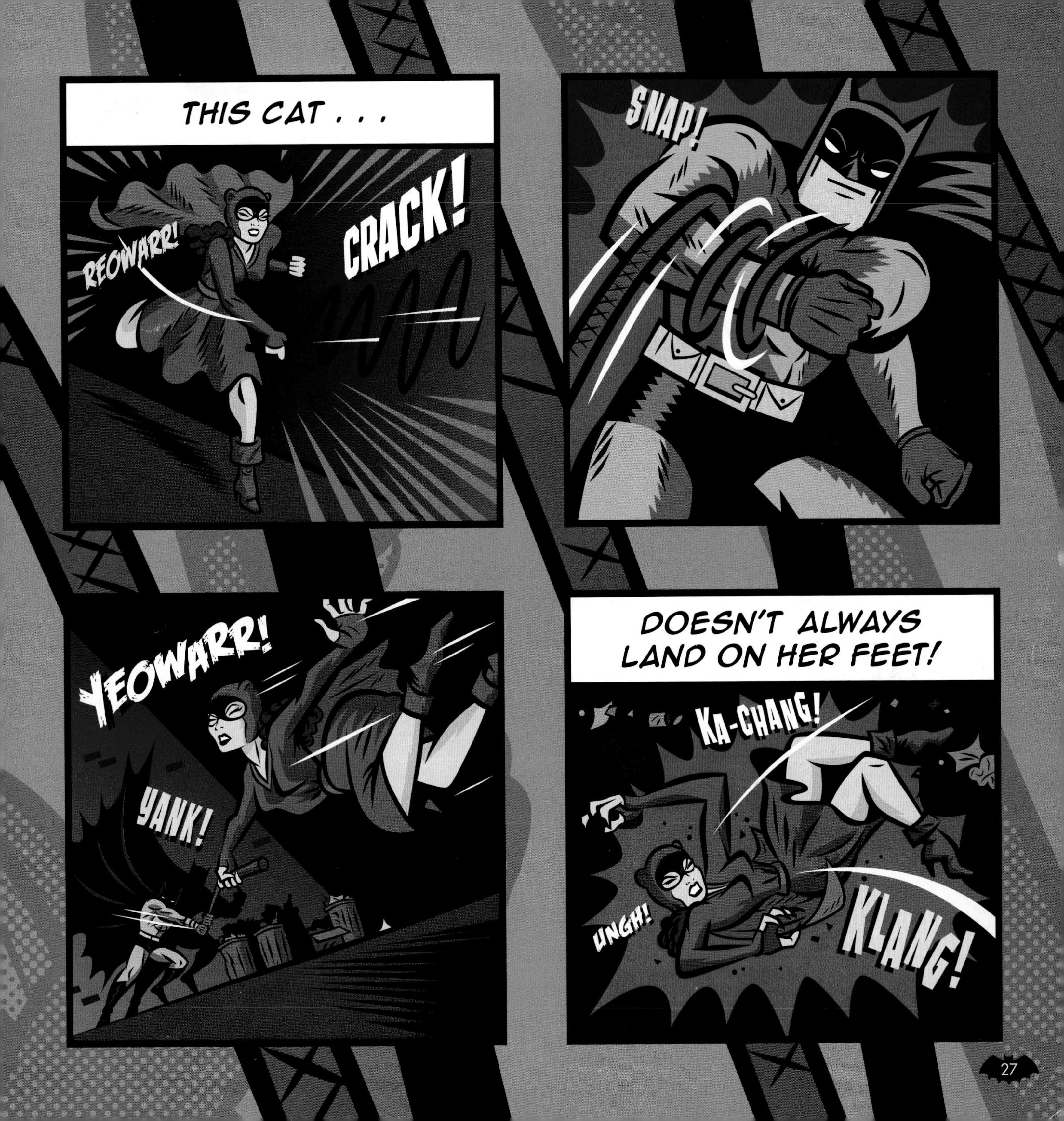
THIS CAT . . .
REOWARR!
CRACK!
SNAP!
YEOWARR!
YANK!
DOESN'T ALWAYS LAND ON HER FEET!
KA-CHANG!
UNGH!
KLANG!

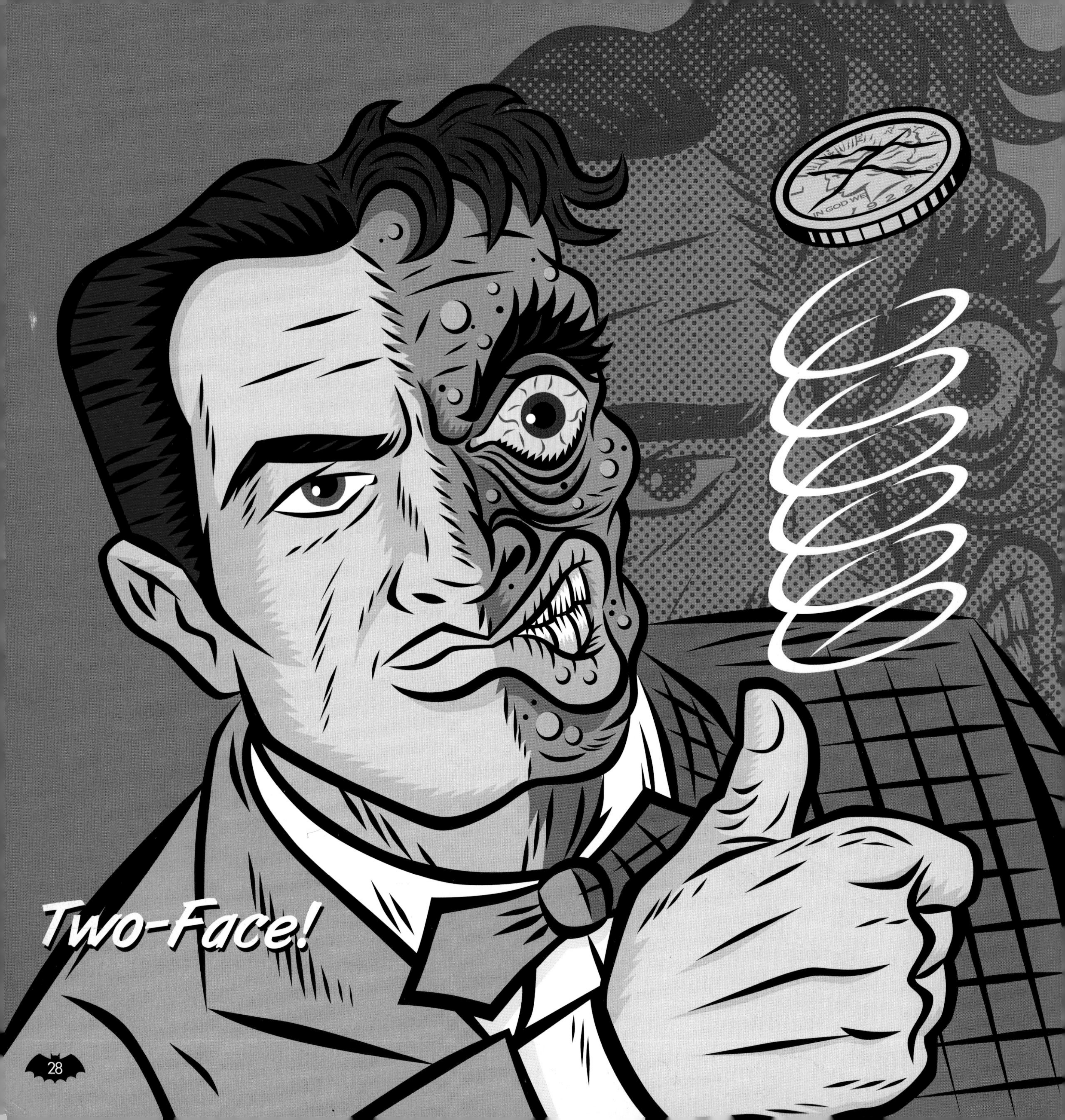
Two-Face!

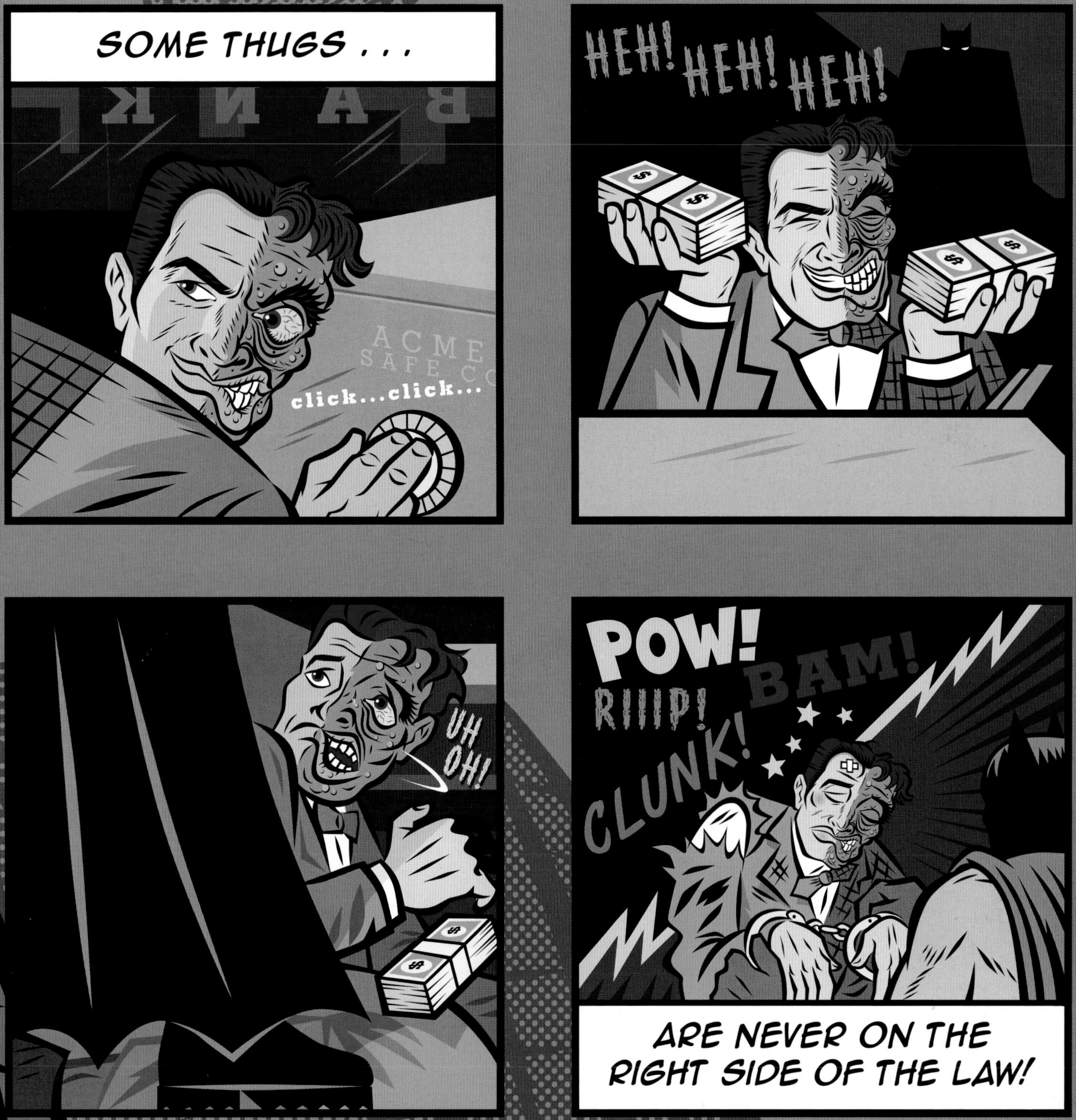
SOME THUGS . . .
BANK
ACME SAFE CO
click...click...
HEH! HEH! HEH!
UH OH!
POW!
RIIIP!
BAM!
CLUNK!
ARE NEVER ON THE RIGHT SIDE OF THE LAW!

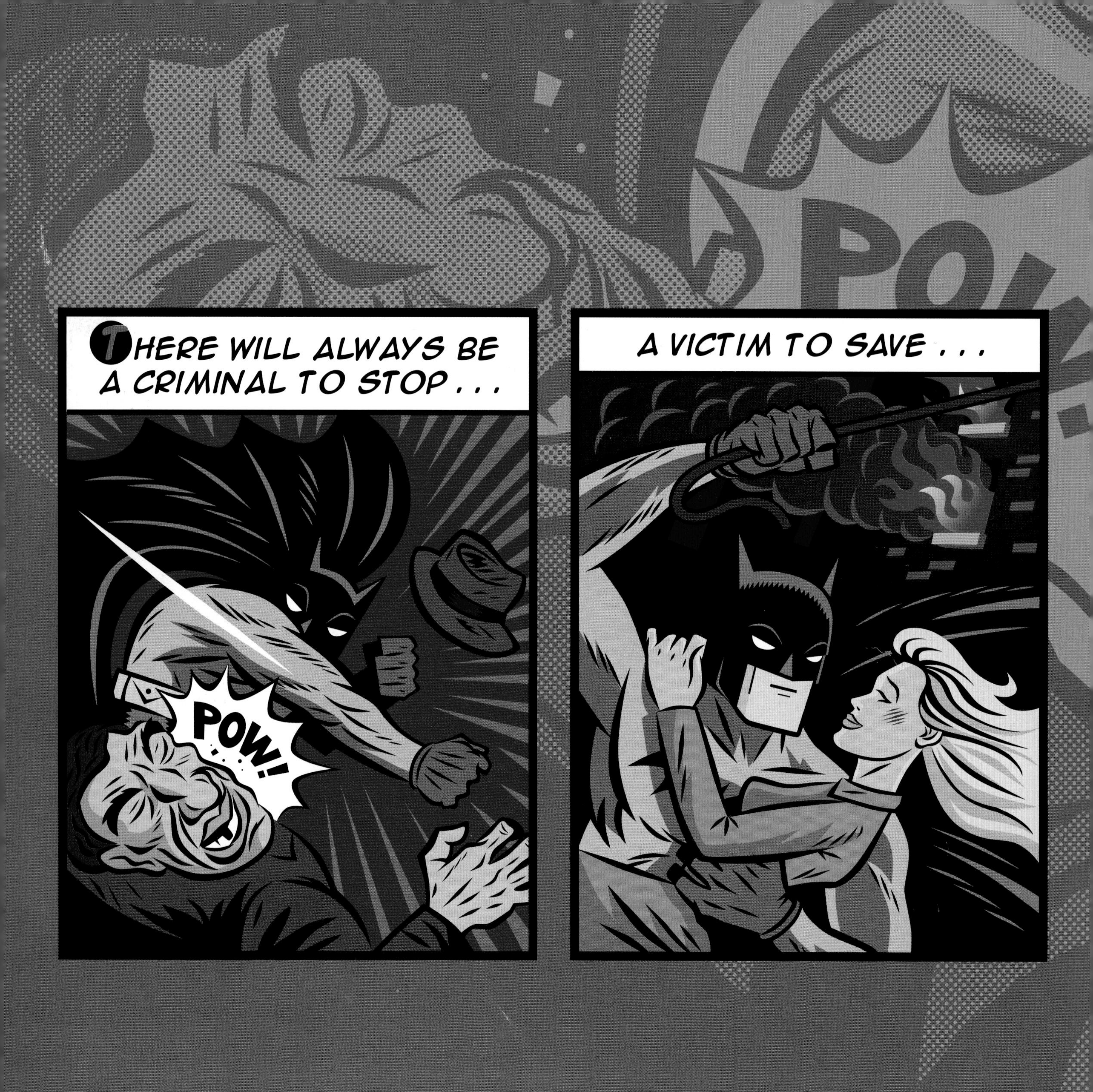
THERE WILL ALWAYS BE A CRIMINAL TO STOP . . .
POW!
A VICTIM TO SAVE . . .

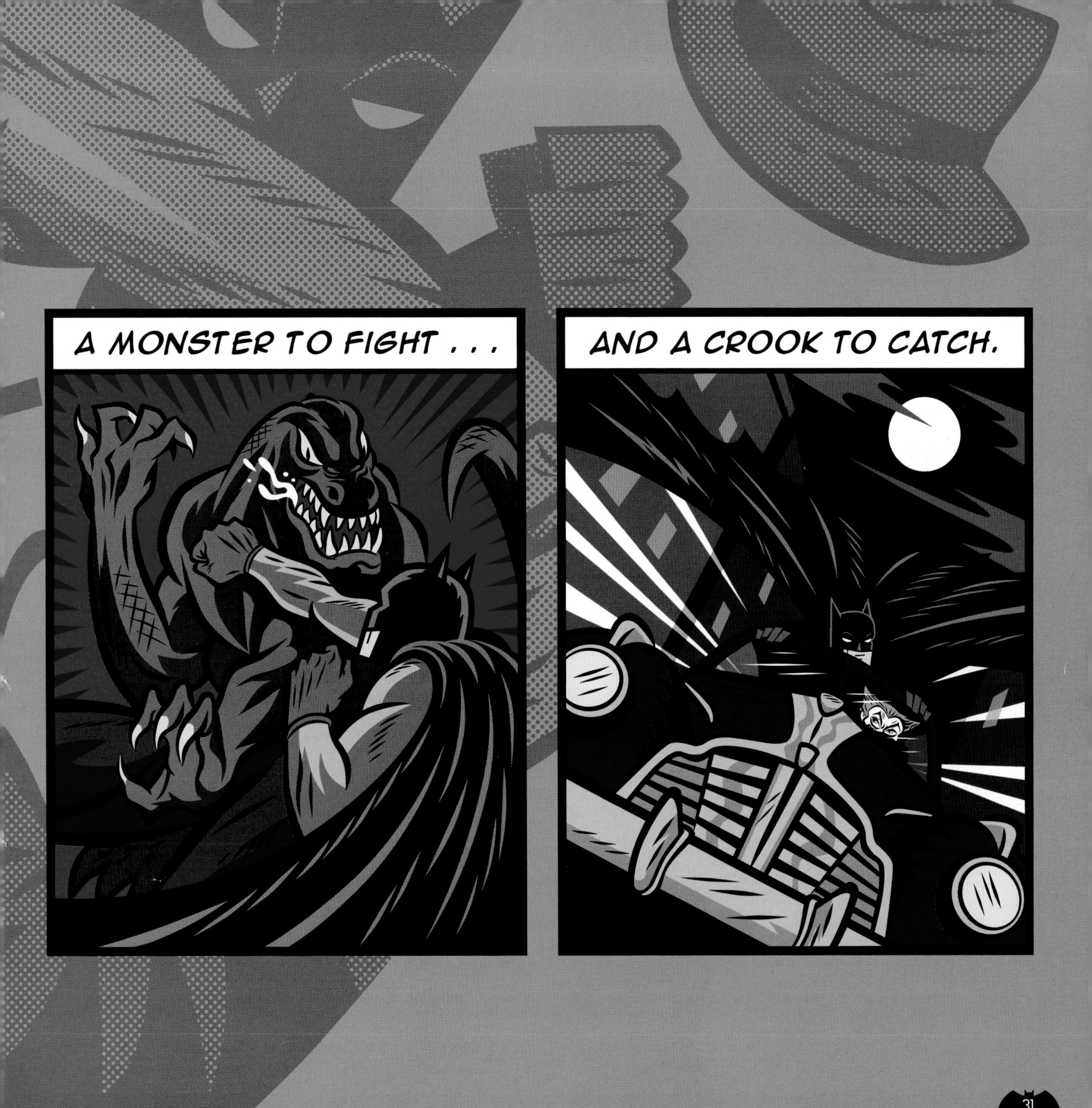
A MONSTER TO FIGHT . . .
AND A CROOK TO CATCH.

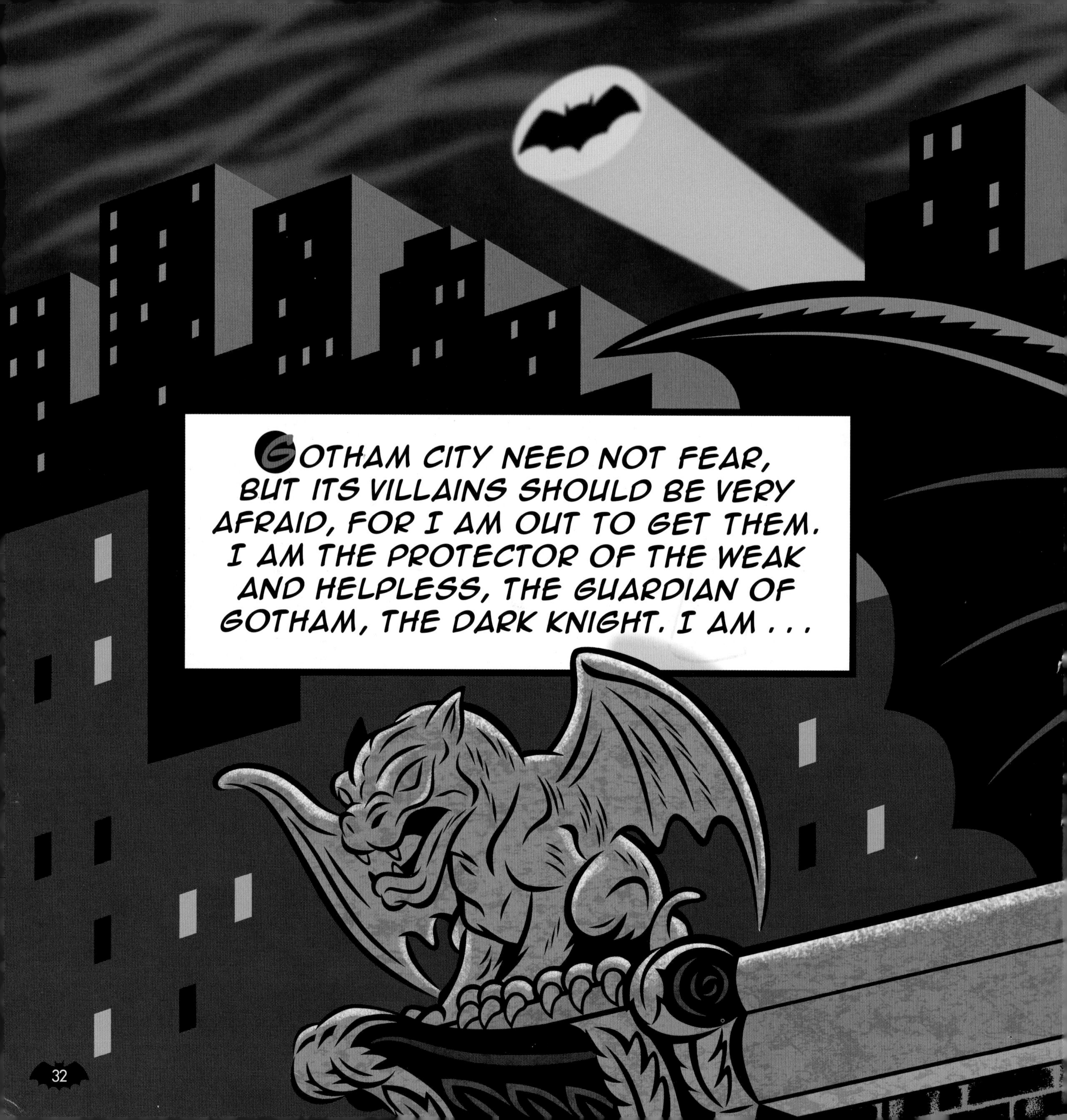
GOTHAM CITY NEED NOT FEAR, BUT ITS VILLAINS SHOULD BE VERY AFRAID, FOR I AM OUT TO GET THEM. I AM THE PROTECTOR OF THE WEAK AND HELPLESS, THE GUARDIAN OF GOTHAM, THE DARK KNIGHT. I AM . . .

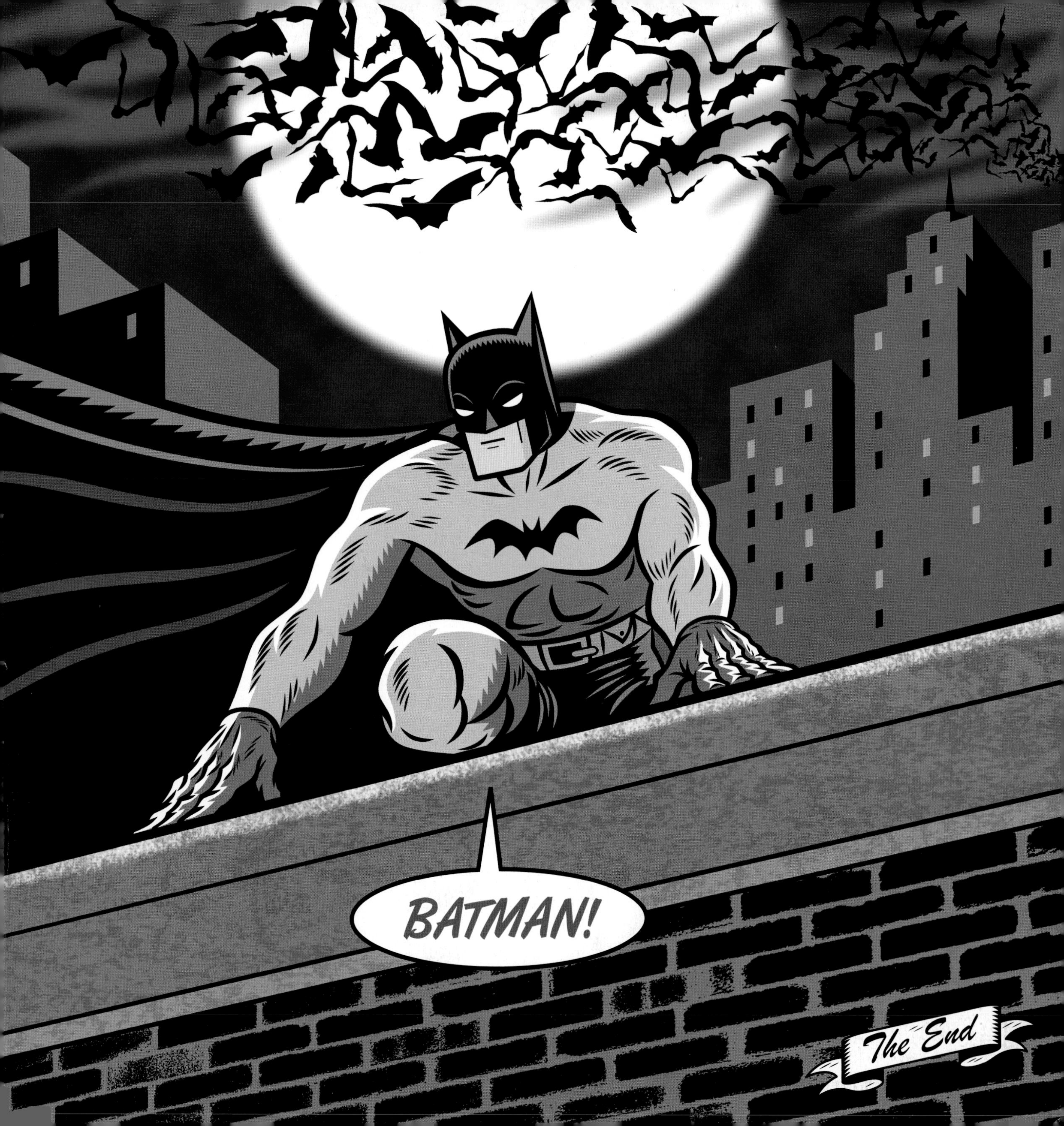
BATMAN!
The End

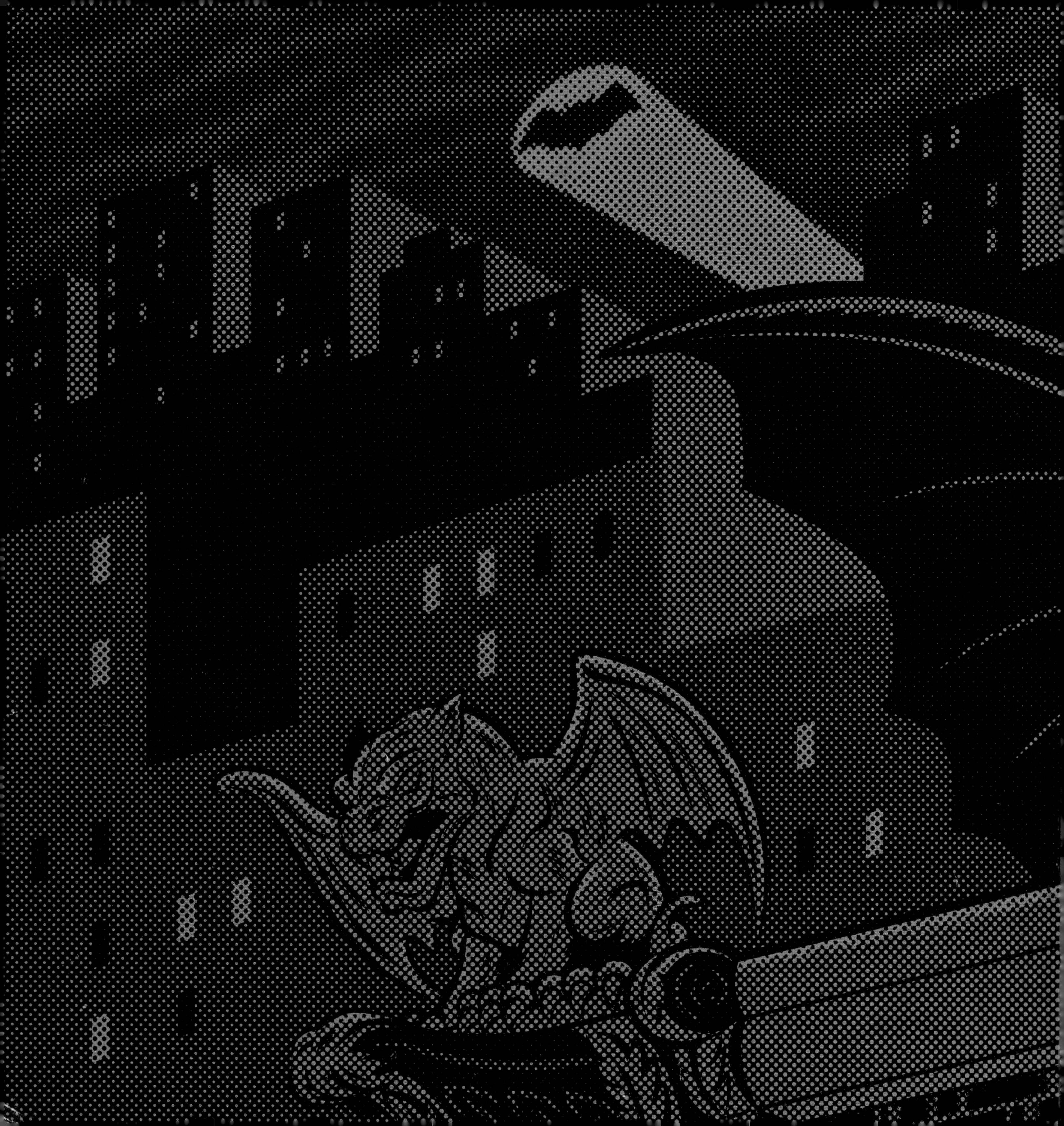